Fic
West
Fri

12.45

D0676923

7.01

SHANNON:
U.S. MARSHAL

SHANNON: U.S. MARSHAL

•

Charles E. Friend

AVALON BOOKS
NEW YORK

PRINTED IN THE UNITED STATES OF AMERICA
ON ACID-FREE PAPER
BY HADDON CRAFTSMEN, BLOOMSBURG, PENNSYLVANIA

My wife Rosemary and I dedicate this book to our friends
Mowgli, Millie, Tuffy, Jenny, and Nunya, who are still with us;
to Sunny, who is dying; and to Smudge, Corky, Peepers,
Sweet Pea, Baby, Penny, Moo, Snowy, Laura, and all
of our other friends who have passed on.
We will not forget them.

Chapter One

The town of Whiskey Creek lay empty and silent, baking in the summer sun. A hot wind was blowing through the streets, carrying clouds of dust before it and driving the inhabitants to seek whatever shelter they could find inside the mining community's weathered wooden buildings. Propelled by the fitful gusts, dust devils swirled along the rutted road that wound up to the hilltop upon which stood Whiskey Creek's version of Boot Hill. The eddies spread fine grey grit between the crooked rows of faded crosses and crudely carved headstones that marked the last resting place of those who had left their dreams and their bones in Whiskey Creek.

Clay Shannon tied his horse to the rusty iron gate at the entrance of the cemetery and made his way slowly through the jumble of markers to a gnarled tree that stood in the far corner. He knelt bareheaded be-

1

side the grave beneath the tree and placed a small bunch of wildflowers at the base of the headstone. Then he reached up and gently brushed away the dust that was slowly obscuring the letters carved into the stone. Shannon had read the words a hundred times, but now he ran his eyes over them again, as if to torment himself with the memories they invoked. The inscription read:

> Katherine Elizabeth Shannon
> Beloved Wife of Clayton Robert Shannon
> and
> Mother of Clayton Robert Shannon, Jr.
> Rest In Peace

Next to his wife's grave was a smaller one. The headstone was smaller also, and the epitaph even more brief.

> Clayton Robert Shannon, Jr.
> Age Four Years

The familiar pain washed over Shannon, tearing at him as it always did. No doubt it was why he visited the graves so seldom now. It had been a year since the outbreak of typhoid fever in Whiskey Creek had taken his wife Kathy, and two years since the brutal murder of their son, but the hurt of their loss had not diminished. Clay Shannon was a strong man, a hard man made even harder by the years he had spent on the American frontier, a place where only the strong and the hard survived. But he had made the mistake of allowing himself one weakness—the love of the little family that now rested on this windy hilltop. And he had paid dearly for that weakness, for the emotional scars left by their loss ran deep within him. Yet tragedy was no stranger to him, for he had seen it often enough in his lifetime, and as he stared at the words on the two headstones, perhaps it was only the blowing dust that made it necessary for him to remove the handkerchief from his pocket and furtively wipe his eyes.

Lost in thought, he suddenly became aware that a voice was calling him from down the hill.

"Sheriff!" cried the voice. "Sheriff Shannon!"

Shannon flicked the rawhide loop off the hammer of his six-gun and rose into a half-crouch, seeking the source of the shouts. Immediately he saw that a young boy was running up the hill toward the cemetery, calling for him. Shannon recognized him as the son of the town's blacksmith, a lad who liked to hang about the sheriff's office and who often ran errands for Shannon and his deputies. Shannon relaxed, moving his hand away from the ivory handle of the Colt revolver at his side.

"Hello, Jimmy," he said. "What's all the fuss about?"

"There's a man waiting for you in your office, Mr. Shannon. He asked me to find you and tell you he's there."

Shannon's eyes narrowed, and he looked searchingly down toward the town. He had few friends and many enemies, and an unknown visitor might or might not be a welcome one.

"Did he tell you his name?" he said, watching the road for any sign of trouble.

"Yessir," said the boy. "He said his name was Rodriguez. He's wearing a badge, Sheriff. I guess he's a lawman just like you."

"Indeed he is," said Shannon, relieved. "Come on, jump up behind my saddle and I'll give you a ride back to town."

Shannon and his passenger dismounted in front of the adobe brick building that served as office and jail. Shannon handed the reins to the boy.

"Will you put him away for me, Jimmy?" he said.

"Sure!" said the boy, thrilled to be entrusted with this important mission. He began to lead the buckskin horse toward the little stable behind the jail. Shannon was already hurrying up the wooden steps and across the covered boardwalk toward the office door, anxious to see Pedro Rodriguez again. Rodriguez had been Shannon's deputy when he first came to Whiskey Creek, and soon had become his friend as well. They had shared the dangerous task of freeing the town from the corrupt and brutal men who had then ruled it. Later, Shannon and Rodriguez had ridden together on the long chase after the killers of Shannon's son. The two had kept in touch even after Rodriguez left Whiskey Creek to become marshal of the town of Dry Wells, some miles to the south, but they had not met since Kathy Shannon's funeral.

The office door was open and Shannon entered, pausing to let his vision adjust to the dim light of the interior. Pedro Rodriguez arose from one of the office's battered wooden chairs and grasped his hand.

"A long time, *amigo*," he said with a grin.

"Too long, Pete," Shannon said. "Sit down and make yourself comfortable. It's good to see you again. How are Maria and the kids?"

"I regret to say that Maria has been ill," said Rodriguez, "but I believe she is on the way to recovery. As for the boys, they are young men now. They ride for some old acquaintances of mine who own a large ranch in New Mexico. And you, my friend, how are you these days?"

"Well enough," Shannon said, looking away.

Rodriguez glanced at the rumpled blankets on the bunk in the corner.

"I see you are sleeping in the office now," he said. "You no longer have that nice little house at the top of the hill?"

"No," said Shannon. "There were too many memories in it. I just couldn't stay there any longer."

"Still, a jail is not a very pleasant place to live," Rodriguez said, looking around the seedy office. "My sympathies, *amigo*. It is a poor reward after all you have done for the people here."

"It doesn't matter," said Shannon indifferently. "I'll be leaving Whiskey Creek soon, probably by the end of the week. The town's dying, Pete. The mines are played out, and people are pulling up stakes every day. The bank and most of the stores have already closed. Soon this will be a ghost town."

"So I have heard," said Rodriguez. "It is sad. So much has happened here, it is hard to think of it end-ing. But then, all things must end, I suppose, sooner or later."

"Yes," said Shannon. "One thing I learned long ago—everything changes, everything dies. It's just a matter of time."

"So what will you do now?" Rodriguez said. "Surely many other towns would be glad to have your services."

"No," said Shannon, "I'm through carrying a star. I talked with Kathy about it once, a couple of years ago. If I'd quit then, she might still be alive today. Now, I've given the town my notice—not that there's much of anyone left to give notice to. In a few days I'll no longer be a lawman. When I leave Whiskey Creek, I'll take only the memories with me. The badge stays behind."

"I'm sorry to hear that you are giving up the law, my friend," Rodriguez said. "How will you live?"

"I've saved up enough to buy a small spread," said Shannon. "A nice little place I first saw many years ago, when I was a deputy city marshal in a nearby town. Who knows—with time and luck I may become a rich cattle baron."

Rodriguez looked thoughtful.

"It is a serious decision," he said, "and only you can make it. You well know that I wish you only the best. But is this the right choice for you? You've been a lawman all your life. I've heard you say a dozen times you'd never do anything else. The law is in your blood, Clay. It is who you are. Can you leave that behind too?"

"I can try," said Shannon darkly.

Rodriguez nodded.

"I understand how you must feel. But before you go, would you do me one last kindness?"

"Anything, Pedro. You know that."

"*Bueno.* I want you to meet a woman. A very special woman. She has accompanied me here for the purpose of talking to you. She is waiting for us at the hotel."

Shannon laughed.

"And just who is this mysterious female, Pete?" he said. "Someone out of your checkered past?"

Rodriguez did not smile. His brown eyes were somber, and he chose his next words carefully.

"Yes," he said, "in a way I suppose she is. She is Charlotte Alvarez, one of the finest ladies I have ever known. Her family owns the ranch in New Mexico that I mentioned a moment ago. It belonged to her father, Don Alejandro Alvarez, and my father was his chief *vaquero*—foreman, as you would say—for many years. I've known Charlotte Alvarez since she was a child, and if I had ever had a daughter I would have wanted her to be just like Charlotte."

"I'm sorry, Pedro," said Shannon, embarrassed. "I didn't mean to make light of it. But why has Señorita Alvarez come here? Why does she want to see me?"

"She is in desperate trouble," Rodriguez replied. "Her father has been murdered, and she and her younger brother are also in great danger. I have brought her here to meet you. She needs your help—badly."

"How can I help her? As I've just said—I'm

through being a lawman. Why did you bring her to me?"

"Because I am one of her oldest friends," Rodriguez said, "and as an old friend she asked me for help. I told her that while I would gladly do anything I could for her, she needed more than I myself could provide. I told her she needed *you*."

Shannon got up and walked to the open doorway to gaze out into the deserted street.

"That's very flattering, Pete," he said, "but I'm afraid I'm going to have to disappoint both of you. Even if I were going to keep on carrying the star, I'm no miracle worker and I don't go riding around the countryside helping ladies in distress. There must be a hundred lawmen in the New Mexico Territory who can do what I could do, and probably do it better."

"You are wrong, *amigo*," Rodriguez said. "No one else will help her. No one. That is why I brought her here to you."

Shannon shook his head in exasperation.

"Then I'm afraid you've wasted your trip, and hers. There's no point even in discussing it with her. I'm sorry."

"My friend," Rodriguez said softly, "I have given her my word that you will speak to her. I beg you not to dishonor me by refusing my request."

Shannon saw that he was trapped.

"All right, Pete," he said tiredly. "I'll see her as a favor to you, and if I can give any advice that might be of use, I'll certainly do so. But what I said still goes—I'm out. In a couple of days this badge comes off and I'll be on my way to becoming a peaceful, happy cattle rancher."

"Of course you are, *amigo*," said Rodriguez, hiding a knowing smile. "Of course you are."

Chapter Two

Pedro Rodriguez had arranged for Señorita Alvarez to have the Whiskey Creek Hotel's one and only suite. It occupied most of the top floor of the three-story building and was known as the "Presidential Suite," but this title was merely a conceit of the hotel management. The rooms had never been occupied by anyone more important than a few visiting mining company executives and a handful of prospectors celebrating their good luck in the gold fields. Pedro rapped gently on the door as Shannon stood behind him, waiting unhappily for an interview he did not expect to enjoy.

"It is I, Pedro," Rodriguez called through the door. "Señor Shannon is with me."

"Please come in, Pedro," said a pleasant female voice from within. Rodriguez opened the door and stepped back to let Shannon enter.

The room, while hardly presidential, was at least clean and well-furnished. A woman stood at the window, silhouetted by the sunlight. As Shannon and Rodriguez entered, she turned and smiled warmly at them.

"Señorita Alvarez," Rodriguez said, "may I present to you Señor Clay Shannon, Sheriff of Whiskey Creek and my very good friend. Clay, this is Señorita Carlota Teresa Isabel Alvarez, of Rancho Alvarez, New Mexico Territory."

"I'm delighted to meet you, Señor Shannon," the woman said, stepping forward and extending her hand. Shannon hesitated, struggling to conceal his surprise. He had pictured a much older woman, probably one clad in some shapeless, dowdy dress. But Charlotte Alvarez was young, certainly well under thirty, with raven black hair and shining brown eyes, and she was dressed in riding clothes that had obviously been tailored by someone who knew how to flatter a female figure. As Shannon reached out to take the proffered hand, it registered on him that this woman was not only young, but also strikingly beautiful.

"An honor, Señorita Alvarez," Shannon gulped, quickly releasing the soft hand.

"Please," she said, "call me Charlotte. It's much less stuffy than that long-winded official title Pedro just reeled off."

Shannon blinked, unable to think of anything intelligent to say. This woman was definitely not what he had expected.

When they were seated, Charlotte Alvarez regarded Shannon searchingly, noting among other things the firm set of his jaw and the well-oiled blue steel Colt revolver resting in the holster on his hip.

"I want to thank you for coming here today, Mr. Shannon," she said. "It was very good of you."

"I was happy to come," Shannon mumbled, somewhat untruthfully.

"I take it that Marshal Rodriguez has explained to you that I have journeyed here searching for someone to assist me," she went on. "My family owns one of the largest cattle ranches in the New Mexico Territory, a tract granted to my ancestors long ago by the King of Spain. When New Mexico became part of the United States, my family elected to stay and become American citizens, and until recently we had no cause to regret that decision."

"Pete—Pedro—has told me something of your troubles," Shannon said. "What exactly has happened?"

"My family's ranch, Rancho Alvarez, is near the town of Los Santos. Last year a man who calls himself 'King' Kruger arrived in Los Santos from the east. He began buying up all the land in the region, often forcing the smaller ranchers out of their holdings by threats and violence. For a time he and his men left us alone, but two months ago he started pressuring my father to sell our estate to him also. My father refused. A week later he was shot to death while riding back to the ranch from Los Santos."

Despite himself, Shannon felt a stir of interest. Violent death was something he understood very well.

"I'm sorry to hear of your loss, Señorita," he said. "I take it that this Kruger was suspected of ordering the killing. Was anyone arrested for the crime?"

"No. Everyone knows that Kruger was behind it. He's even bragged about it openly. But the county sheriff is in Kruger's pay, and so naturally nothing was ever done."

Shannon frowned. It was a familiar story. As a lawman, he had encountered similar situations many times, but it still disturbed him to hear of such things. For the most part Shannon was a tolerant man, but he deeply detested the outlaws he hunted, the thieves and murderers who preyed upon those weaker than themselves, and he despised even more the corrupt peace officers who dishonored their profession by protecting the guilty from the consequences of their crimes—or by committing those crimes themselves. For such men he had no tolerance at all.

"I think I understand the situation," he said. "And now?"

"My mother died some years ago, so since our father's death the ranch belongs to my brother, Diego, and me. Kruger has demanded that we sell our land to him for a pittance, the land that has been my family's home for generations, and the lovely house in which my brother and I were born and have lived all our lives. Naturally, we have refused to sell."

"And what's happened since your refusal?" Shannon said. "Have you been threatened?"

"More than threatened. Many of our cattle have been stolen, and several of our *vaqueros* have been attacked. One of them, a man who has worked for us for many years, was caught alone out on the range. They beat him savagely and then sent him back to us wrapped in barbed wire cut from one of our own fences. They told him it was a warning to our other employees to seek work elsewhere. Then, just a week ago, Kruger and his men stopped my carriage on the road from Los Santos. My driver and I tried to defend ourselves, but there were too many of them. The driver was knocked senseless and I was held at gunpoint. I was not harmed, but Kruger warned me that if I did not agree within the week to sell him the ranch, the same fate that befell my father would be suffered by my brother and me."

"Not a very subtle fellow, is he?" said Shannon.

"Tell him the rest," Rodriguez said.

She looked down at her hands where they lay folded in her lap.

"Then Kruger ordered his *pistoleros* to shoot my horses, my beautiful horses that I raised from foals, just to emphasize his threat. After that they all rode away laughing, leaving me alone on the road with the injured man. The land is very dry and desolate there, and as you well know, anyone left afoot without water in country like that is at great risk. Had not my brother noted my long absence from the hacienda and sent out a search party for me, things might have gone very badly indeed. I was fortunate—that time. But I have no doubt that Kruger will carry out his threats if Diego and I do not surrender Rancho Alvarez to him."

"But surely your riders can protect you and your home from these men?"

"We have only a handful of *vaqueros* now," she said sadly. "Many of our people have left us, frightened away by the threats."

"Don't the good citizens of Los Santos object to all this? Won't they help you stand up to Kruger?"

Charlotte Alvarez shook her head, and when she spoke Shannon could hear the sorrow in her voice.

"No, Señor Shannon, they will not," she said. "Many of the people of Los Santos despise Kruger, but they will not interfere with him."

Her expression became wistful.

"Once," she went on, "before the annexation by the United States of the New Mexico Territory, our family was rich and influential, perhaps the most influential in the region. But since the *Anglos* have gained power in our part of the Territory, our position has become quite different. Like other families in the region who are of Spanish descent, we have little influence now, and very few friends. It is for this reason that Kruger can threaten and brutalize and murder us without fear of punishment. The residents of Los Santos are terrified of him. There have been not only threats, but also vicious assaults on people who have spoken out against him. Wives and children have been terrorized, and a few mornings ago one of the townspeople who had tried to organize resistance against Kruger was found dead, hanged from the limb of a tree right in the plaza. Nothing was done about that either. No, Señor Shannon, the people will not help us. They cannot even help themselves."

Anger had been rising up in Shannon as he listened to this painful account. However, he forced himself to stifle his indignation, for he knew from experience that he must not let his emotions cloud his judgment. This was a time for clear thinking. Reviewing the woman's story in his mind, it occurred to him that there was something missing, something else that had not yet been mentioned.

"It seems to me," he said slowly, "that your friend Kruger is going to great lengths to gain control of an area that is, by your own description, dry and desolate. Why does Kruger want all of this land so much?"

"I don't know," she said. "I wish I did, because then I might know better how to resist him. It may be simple greed, or perhaps it is the lust for power that afflicts so many men. Or there may be some other reason. Kruger despises our people, the *Mexicanos*, and so hatred alone may be his motive—I cannot say. Or it may be that he just pretends to hate us, to gain the support of the *Anglos* who would like to see us driven out. But whatever his motives, one thing is certain—he will do anything to get what he wants. Anything. He is like a wild animal, and unless someone stops him soon, we are lost."

She leaned forward in her chair, her face tense and her eyes fixed unwaveringly upon Shannon.

"That is why I have come to you, Señor Shannon," she said. "I have heard from Señor Rodriguez, and from others as well, that you are a brave and honest man, a man who is not afraid to risk his life to help others. So now I ask you—will you help *me*?"

Shannon got up and moved to the window. Below him the main street of Whiskey Creek lay smothered in its own dust. A team of sweating horses was hauling a heavily loaded wagon past the hotel, a man and a woman on the seat and three children in the back. *Another family leaving town*, Shannon thought to himself. *Another nail in Whiskey Creek's coffin. It won't be long now*. He glanced down at the star pinned to his shirt, the star he had worn so long. Soon it would mean nothing to him, and the thought saddened him.

But, he reminded himself, his personal problems were irrelevant at the moment. He was facing a dilemma he had not anticipated. He had come to the hotel as a favor to Pedro Rodriguez, fully expecting a boring conversation and an automatic refusal of the unknown woman's request. He did not want to get involved in anyone else's troubles just then. He wanted to hand in his badge and hang up his gun and ride away to the little ranch that was waiting for him. Nevertheless, he was moved by Charlotte Alvarez's story—not because of her beauty, although many men might have been swayed by it—but simply because she was the victim of a great injustice, and fighting against injustice had been Shannon's life. He would like to assist her, even if it meant postponing his own plans. But there was one irremediable aspect of the situation that made it impossible.

He turned to face her.

"I'm sorry," he said with genuine regret. "I wish I could help you, but there are several reasons why I can't. The first is that I've made other plans, plans that are important to me. I've already explained this to Marshal Rodriguez."

He moved over to her chair and stood above her as she sat looking up at him.

"The second reason, Señorita Alvarez, is that I am not the man you suppose me to be. I hope I'm honest, and I think I can handle a six-gun as well as most men, but I'm not particularly brave and I doubt that I have any of the other virtues that Pedro has apparently so generously attributed to me."

Pedro Rodriguez opened his mouth to say something, but Shannon silenced him with a wave of his hand.

"Most important of all, Señorita," he continued, "I'm a professional lawman, and have been all my adult life. During all those years I've always—well, almost always—acted only by virtue of lawful authority, the authority vested in me by the jurisdiction I serve. That's what it means to be a peace officer, to take the oath, to carry the star. But you're asking me to go to a place where I have no authority at all, to ride into a situation where I'd be nothing but another *pistolero*, a man outside the law, a paid gunslinger no better than the killers who work for your Mr. Kruger. There are many men in the West whose guns are for sale to the highest bidder, whoever it may be. I'm not one of those men. My gun is not for sale, not even in a cause as worthy as yours. I hope you'll forgive me for speaking so bluntly, but I want you to understand why I must refuse your request."

Shannon paused, watching her, dreading the hurt and disappointment that he knew must now appear in her dark eyes. Instead, he found himself subjected to one of the greatest surprises of his life. Charlotte Alvarez looked at Rodriguez, pleasure lighting her face.

"Pedro, my old friend," she said, "you haven't exaggerated Señor Shannon's qualities. Beyond doubt this is the man I need, and most definitely the man I want. Thank you for bringing me to him."

Shannon stood there in astonishment for a full ten seconds as she smiled up at him. He began to fumble for words, convinced that she had misunderstood his statements and taken his refusal for an acceptance. But Pedro Rodriguez was smiling also, a self-satisfied smile that Shannon found incomprehensible. Had these people taken leave of their senses? Had he failed so miserably to convey his decision to them?

"Do not look so perplexed, *amigo*," Rodriguez said. "I have known you for a long time, and Señorita Alvarez and I fully anticipated the objection you have just stated. But there is something else you must hear. Señorita, will you do the honors?"

Charlotte Alvarez rose from her chair and moved to a small table that stood nearby. On the table was a folded piece of paper. She picked it up and faced Shannon.

"I'm afraid we haven't been entirely open with you, Mr. Shannon," she said gently. "I said that my family now has little influence and few friends, and that is certainly true. But we do have one friend remaining to us who is willing to help, and he is, fortunately for us, the Territorial Governor. There is little that even he can do for us, but he has at least been able to do this much. He has obtained this document for us—and for you."

"What is it?" Shannon asked, a little annoyed. Couldn't this woman take no for an answer?

Charlotte Alvarez's smile was triumphant.

"Señor Shannon," she said, "it is your appointment as deputy United States marshal for the Territory of New Mexico."

"My *what*?" said Shannon, dumbfounded.

She held out the paper to him.

"There is your lawful authority, Mr. Shannon," she said. "You are now a federal officer, legally empowered to enforce the laws of the United States and of New Mexico—however, wherever, and whenever you may wish."

Shannon took the paper from her and read it, still stunned.

"But . . . but . . ." he stammered, looking helplessly at her.

Rodriguez chuckled at Shannon's discomfort.

"Here," he said. "I think this will help."

He withdrew a shining badge from his shirt pocket and placed it in Shannon's palm.

"We took the precaution of bringing this with us," Rodriguez said. "Charlotte received it from the Governor's own hand. It's official, Clay. You will *not* be just a 'hired gun,' nor would we have asked you to be. It's 'Shannon, U.S. Marshal' now. The Governor has arranged that this honor be conferred upon you, and a well-deserved honor it is. Congratulations, *amigo*."

Shannon stared at the bright star nestled in his hand, a dozen conflicting emotions filling his mind. Then, suddenly, elation flooded through him. If he accepted this appointment, he would not have to give up his profession after all. He would still be a lawman, and a federal lawman at that. He would have one more chance to do the things that mattered most to him— to uphold the law, to bring criminals to justice, to save innocent victims from the acts of ruthless and violent men. Instantly the anger, the sorrow, the hopelessness, and the black depression that had filled his heart and soul during the past days were washed away. In that moment he became new and clean and young again, and, like any true hunter, he felt the old excitement, the thrill of the chase, beginning to stir within him.

Then a thought struck him.

"I'll give you my answer within the hour," he said. "Before I decide, there's someone I have to talk to."

Charlotte Alvarez looked at him questioningly, waiting for an explanation, but Pedro Rodriguez merely smiled and nodded. He knew who it was that Shannon was going to see.

Chapter Three

For the second time that day, Shannon knelt beside his wife's grave. The wildflowers he had placed there that same morning were now wilting in the heat and already half-scattered by the relentless wind. He knew that when he left Whiskey Creek, her grave and his son's would be untended. The weeds would spring up and the sand drift in, erasing all evidence of their existence.

"I wish you were here, Kathy," he whispered. "I wish I knew what you'd want me to do."

He thought back to the evening long ago when Kathy and Bobby and he had sat at the table in their little kitchen, eating and laughing and sharing the warmth of their love. It was the last time they would be together, for the next day a cruel enemy from Shannon's past had ridden into Whiskey Creek and taken Bobby from him forever. But on that last night he had told

Kathy that he was thinking of resigning, and he remembered her reply as clearly as if it had been yesterday.

"You must do as you think best, Clay," she had said. "If that's what you want, it's fine with me. But are you sure it's the right thing for you to do? For yourself, I mean. You told me once you'd never stop carrying the star, as you call it, because that's all you've ever done."

Strange, he said to himself. *Those are almost the same words that Pedro Rodriguez said to me two hours ago.*

He looked out across the valley at the hills on the horizon, the low hills that he had seen a thousand times before.

You were wise, Kathy, he thought. *Wiser than I. You knew me better than I knew myself. I'll never quit the law. Pedro was right—it's who I am. And it's who we were, you and I. You told me that then, and I think you're telling me that now. And I won't disappoint you.*

He brushed the eternal dust from the tombstone and carefully rearranged the flowers once more. Then he got to his feet and stood there for a moment, looking down at the two little plots of earth that held all that was left of his family.

He reached up and unpinned the sheriff's badge and slipped it into his pocket. Then he took out the deputy U.S. marshal's star and fastened it securely to his shirt.

"Goodbye, Kathy," he said quietly. "Thank you."

He mounted the buckskin and rode slowly down the hill to the hotel. Pedro Rodriguez opened the door of the suite as soon as Shannon knocked. Charlotte Alvarez sat in the same chair as before. She looked at him expectantly, awaiting his answer.

"All right, people," Shannon said gruffly. "When do we leave for New Mexico?"

They decided that they would set out early the following morning. Shannon spent the rest of the day making his preparations for the trip. He had already given notice of his resignation, but he took the time to visit several of the remaining citizens of Whiskey Creek to tell them he was leaving. Most seemed to have little interest, since they were busy preparing for their own departure.

One exception was Doctor McCallum, the man who had attended Shannon's son as he lay dying. Shannon found McCallum in the medical office attached to his home. The door to the little room behind the office was open, and as Shannon said his goodbyes to Doctor and Mrs. McCallum, he could not help but glance through the doorway at the bed on which his son had died. He quickly looked away.

"I hate to see you go, Clay," McCallum said. "You've done so much here. When you came to Whiskey Creek it was just another wild, lawless mining town. You made it safe for people to walk the streets, made this the good place to live that it came to be. I wish you had received a better reward for your work. You've gotten little pay and little thanks from the community that owes you so much."

"That goes with the job, Doc," Shannon said. "Anyway, I don't regret anything. I had some good years here with my family. Those years are over now, and it's time to move on. What about you? Where will you go?"

"There's always room for another doctor somewhere,' " McCallum said with a laugh. "There'll always be somebody's bullet holes to patch up, and somebody's babies to be delivered. I'll stay on here in Whiskey Creek for a little while, though, until everyone else has left and there's no longer any need for me."

"Doc," Shannon said, "until you leave, would you look after the graves of my wife and son? Just visit them occasionally, keep the weeds away, that sort of thing?"

"I'll be glad to," McCallum said. He patted Shannon's arm. "Don't carry too much bitterness with you, Clay," he added. "What's done is done. Your wife and boy are gone, and nothing can change that. But you have a whole new life before you now—enjoy it. Look forward, not back. Live for each new day and don't let any moment be spoiled by thoughts of the past. Don't carry the bad memories away with you, only the good ones."

"I'll try, Doc," Shannon said, "but some of the things that happened here won't be easy to forget."

"Well, good luck to you," the doctor said, shaking his hand. "Stay well and be happy."

"I'll try to be happy," Shannon said, "but whether I'll stay well depends on the marksmanship of all the people who'll probably be shooting at me."

* * *

Shannon collected his belongings and carefully packed them for his departure. There was little enough to pack. The contents of the house on the hill had been sold along with the house itself, for Shannon did not want to hold on to the memories they invoked. Beyond that, he had only his clothes, his weapons, and his horse. Clay Shannon was leaving Whiskey Creek as he had arrived in it—a lonely man with all his worldly goods neatly tucked into two small saddlebags.

He had already made the necessary arrangements to close up the sheriff's office and pay off his last remaining deputy. He passed his final evening in the office cleaning out his desk, alone with the shadows cast by the oil lamp and the ghosts that haunted that dark little place.

He could have stayed in the hotel overnight, but instead he elected to sleep in the office one last time. He spent a restless night on the bunk, thinking about what he was leaving behind and wondering what lay ahead.

The next morning he arose at dawn, shaved and dressed, and put the last of his personal things into the saddlebags. He closed the shutters on the office windows and looked around to see if he had missed anything. Everything seemed in order. Finally, he took the Whiskey Creek sheriff's badge out of his pocket and laid it carefully on the empty desktop.

He carried his saddlebags out the door and threw them over the back of his waiting horse. The buckskin shied nervously at the unfamiliar weight. Shannon calmed the animal and went back to the door of the office. He took one last glance at the shabby room in which he had spent so many years. *McCallum says I should take only the good memories with me*, Shannon reminded himself. *Good advice, but can I do it?* Reluctantly, he closed the door that was the exit from the office and from his past. He locked the door and hung the key on a nail beside the doorframe, in case anyone should need to get in.

Then he walked the horse down the hill to the livery stable. Despite his best efforts, the memories, good and bad, followed him.

As planned, Pedro Rodriguez and Charlotte Alvarez were waiting for him at the stable, their horses already saddled. The three of them left Whiskey Creek just as the sun rose over the distant mountains into the eastern sky. They splashed through the stream that had given the town its name and moved out across the little valley beyond. At the top of the next rise, Shannon reined in the buckskin and looked back. Whiskey Creek's wooden buildings clung precariously to the steep slopes, just as they had done eight years before when he first arrived. There were more buildings now, but they still looked as dilapidated as ever, and the empty streets gave the place an eerie quality of desolation. Shannon gazed at the town one last time, then turned and rode slowly over the crest of the hill, into the unknown.

Chapter Four

They traveled first to Dry Wells, where Pedro Rodriguez served as city marshal. There was little conversation between them during the journey, for they were all thinking of what the coming days might bring. Shannon noted with approval that Charlotte Alvarez was an excellent rider, gentle but firm with her spirited grey horse. The hardships of the trail did not seem to affect her at all. When the sun grew hot and the choking dust blew up around them, she made no complaint, and when they stopped occasionally to rest and water the horses, she was always the first one back in the saddle. Shannon found himself admiring both her stamina and her determination.

They arrived in Dry Wells near dusk, tired by the ride but eager to get on with the next part of the journey. Shannon and Charlotte Alvarez took overnight rooms at the town's only hotel, while Pedro hurried home to see his wife. An hour later he joined his two companions as they were eating an uninspiring dinner in the hotel's dining room. As Rodriguez approached, Shannon could see from his expression that he was troubled.

"How's Maria?" Shannon asked as his friend sat down at the table.

"Not well," Rodriguez said. "A fever of some sort. The doctor is with her now. He says that other people here are suffering from a similar sickness."

Shannon felt his stomach turn over. When typhoid fever had struck Whiskey Creek, his own wife had fallen victim to the disease while trying to nurse others back to health. He could only hope for his friend's sake that Maria Rodriguez would not meet a similar fate.

"I trust it's not . . . not the same thing we had in Whiskey Creek," he said hesitantly. He could not bring himself to utter the word "typhoid."

"I don't think it is," said Rodriguez, looking sharply at Shannon. He knew full well how Kathy Shannon had died, and how much Shannon dreaded a repetition of that tragedy. "Don't worry, my friend," Rodriguez said soothingly. "The symptoms are different, and although the fever is bad, no one has yet perished from it. Maria is strong. I am confident that she will recover."

"You must stay here with her until she's well," Shannon said.

"Yes," said Charlotte. "She needs you now. When she has recovered, you can join us in Los Santos."

Rodriguez looked doubtfully at Shannon.

"You will need me in New Mexico, *amigo*," he said. "It is my duty to go with you. After all, it was I who brought you into this."

"Stay with Maria, Pedro," Shannon said. "Follow us when you can. By the time you arrive, I'll know more about the situation and we can decide what to do then. Meanwhile, family comes first. Do you agree, Señorita Alvarez?"

"Absolutely," she said, placing her hand on Rodriguez's arm. "Stay, Pedro. We'll meet you in Los Santos."

Rodriguez sighed.

"You're right, of course," he said. "But I will be much happier when Maria is well again and you and I are together once more. In the meantime, take care, my friends. Do not underestimate this fellow Kruger."

"I never underestimate a mad dog," said Shannon.

The next morning Shannon and Charlotte Alvarez boarded the stagecoach that would take them to Santa Fe, where they would catch another stage that would carry them on to Los Santos. Shannon was not happy about leaving his beloved buckskin horse behind in order to ride in the noisy, confined, and odoriferous interior of a bouncing stagecoach, but he had little choice. Speed was essential, for they had all agreed that Shannon and Charlotte must get to the Alvarez ranch before Kruger made his next move, and it was many miles to Los Santos. The stage lines could carry them there long before they could make the trip on horseback.

"I'll take good care of the buckskin for you," Pedro promised, "and I'll bring him with me when I come."

"Don't feed him too much," Shannon said. "He's a big eater, and I don't want to have to chase after Kruger on a fat horse."

The stagecoach rattled southward at a steady clip. The country through which they passed was vast and barren. Shannon watched through the coach's open windows as they climbed laboriously up through the mountain passes and rolled out across the high, arid plains. Although Shannon and Charlotte Alvarez were the only passengers, the noise and the dust and the general discomfort of the journey discouraged conversation. Shannon was grateful for this, for now that Pedro Rodriguez was not with them, he found himself strangely ill at ease in Charlotte's presence. Why this should be so he wasn't sure, for she was beyond question a warm and gracious person, and he knew she sensed his reticence and was doing everything she could to put him at his ease.

Perhaps it's because she's so attractive, Shannon thought. *There hasn't been anyone since Kathy, and I've forgotten how to talk to a beautiful woman.* She had curled up in one corner of the seat opposite him, and had eventually dozed off despite the uncomfortable motion of the stagecoach. He studied her thoughtfully as she slept, wondering about her, about what she was really like, and above all about how well she would face up to the ugliness that inevitably lay ahead of them. Her outward manner was calm and feminine, but beneath the calmness and the soft femininity Shannon detected steel. He decided that, based upon what he had seen of her so far, she was the kind of woman who would be a good friend, a faithful and passionate lover—and a very, very dangerous enemy.

Kruger, he thought, *no matter how tough you are, I think you made a big mistake when you took on Charlotte Alvarez.*

Despite the steady pace, the stage was late getting into Santa Fe, and there was barely time to eat a hasty meal before the departure of the coach for Los Santos. Shannon had never been to Santa Fe before, and he was fascinated by it. The town retained the distinctive Latin character that one would expect of a community with a proud Spanish heritage. Shannon decided that he was going to like New Mexico.

He became less sure of his conclusion when he saw the Los Santos stagecoach. The vehicle was old and battered; indeed, it appeared to be on the point of disintegration. However, the driver and shotgun guard were *Mexicanos*, and they ushered Charlotte Alvarez aboard with all the deference due to the daughter of an old and revered Spanish family.

Shannon made sure that their belongings, including his Winchester rifle, had been securely transferred from the other stagecoach to the Los Santos stage. Then, when Charlotte was safely aboard, he took a seat beside her. Despite his appreciation of Santa Fe, he was experiencing a growing feeling of apprehension, as if some sixth sense were warning him that all was not well. Unobtrusively, so as not to alarm his traveling companion, he undid the hammer loop on his holster and checked the cylinder of the Colt to make sure that it was fully loaded and spun freely. It was with some amusement that, as he slid the six-gun back into the holster, he looked up and saw that Charlotte Alvarez was just completing a similar inspection of a small silver .32 caliber revolver she had produced from inside her jacket.

"What are you grinning about, Mr. Shannon?" she said with a mischievous smile.

"Oh, nothing," said Shannon innocently. "It's just that I couldn't help noticing your unusual jewelry. Pardon me for asking, Señorita, but do you know how to use that thing?"

She smiled at him, but behind the laughing eyes Shannon caught a glimpse of the steel he had suspected.

"You can count on it, Marshal," she said. Shannon believed her.

This time they were not the only passengers. As they sat in the stagecoach waiting for it to depart for Los Santos, a plump man in a checkered suit struggled up the steps of the coach and collapsed, perspiring freely, on the seat opposite Shannon and Charlotte.

"Howdy, folks," he said, wiping his face with a crumpled handkerchief. "Josiah Ames is the name. Just out from St. Louis. I'm a whiskey drummer, as you can see."

He held up the battered black case he was carrying.

"Care for a sample, ma'am? Sir?"

"Thank you, no," said Charlotte. Shannon shook his head without answering and gazed pointedly out the window. Somewhat chastened by this cool reception, Ames sat back in the seat and began to fidget.

As the stage was about to pull out, a tall, thin man in a black suit, white shirt, and black string tie climbed into the coach and sat down next to the whiskey drummer, facing Shannon and Charlotte Alvarez.

Shannon studied the newcomer with a professional eye. The man did not introduce himself, and indeed at first he did not speak at all. Shannon decided that he had all the earmarks of a professional gambler. Shannon had no prejudices against gamblers—at least not the honest ones—but there was something else about this man, something that Shannon found mildly disturbing. Among other things, the stranger had the most piercing eyes he had ever seen. They were as yellow as a cat's eyes, and they gazed coldly back at Shannon for a long moment as the two men took each other's measure. Then a hint of wry humor touched the stranger's gaunt face, as if he had thought of some private joke. He nodded to Charlotte, said, "Your servant, ma'am," and looked away out the window.

Those are a gunfighter's eyes, Shannon thought. *I wonder if this fellow is one of King Kruger's hired killers. And, if so, I wonder if he knows who we are. This could be an interesting trip.*

The country through which they were traveling was stark and broken. Rocky cliffs and deep arroyos flanked the road, and the only plant life to be seen was dry brush and cactus. The sun soon reached the zenith and began its descent to the western horizon, sending lengthening shadows crawling out toward the passing stagecoach. The hours dragged by slowly, and eventually the whiskey drummer, out of sheer boredom, began a long monologue on the vicissitudes of his trade. Charlotte listened politely, but Shannon and the black-clad stranger ignored him. The stranger had said nothing further since they left Santa Fe, and Shannon was becoming irritated by his detachment.

"What time do you think we'll reach Los Santos?" he said loudly, watching for the man's reaction. Shannon knew perfectly well what time the stage was supposed to arrive, but he wanted to do something to jar the stranger out of his long, silent study of the scenery.

The cold eyes examined Shannon without emotion.

"That's hard to say," the stranger said. "On a journey like this, many things can happen."

The statement proved to be a prophecy. Shannon was still digesting the stranger's answer when gunfire erupted from the rocks on the left side of the road. Splinters flew into the interior of the coach as bullets smashed through the wooden sides, narrowly missing the occupants. Out of the nearest arroyo seven or eight horsemen appeared at full gallop, paralleling the road and firing repeating rifles at the stage. The attackers were clad only in breechclouts, and their faces were covered with war paint.

"Indians!" Ames squeaked, hugging his sample case as if to protect it from being scalped.

The stage driver whipped the team into a full gallop, and the boom of a shotgun sounded from above them as the guard opened fire from his perch on the boot. Shannon put his arm around Charlotte Alvarez and pushed her down onto the floor of the coach.

"Stay there!" he shouted, drawing his six-gun.

Another volley of shots crashed into the stage, and Shannon heard the sickening sound of a bullet striking flesh. Josiah Ames gasped and collapsed against the wall of the coach, his jaw hanging open. There was a startled expression on his face, as if he had been un-pleasantly surprised by the small, dark hole that had just appeared in the side of his head.

Shannon leaned out one of the coach windows and took careful aim at the nearest of the painted riders. He fired, and the man tumbled off the horse, flopping over and over in the dust as the animal galloped away from him.

"Excellent shot, Mr. Shannon," said the stranger. From inside his coat he produced a gold-engraved black revolver and began to fire coolly—almost dis-interestedly—out the window nearest him. As he fired, first one and then another of the riders threw up his arms and went plummeting out of the saddle onto the hard sand.

Shannon had no time to ponder the fact that the stranger had spoken his name. The remaining attackers were still shooting at them, and Shannon was absorbed in returning their fire. A pistol cracked beside him, and he saw that Charlotte Alvarez was firing back also. *Good for you, Charlotte*, thought Shannon. *But don't forget to save the last one for yourself.*

A scream issued from the top of the stagecoach, and the body of the driver tumbled down past Shannon's window into the road. The coach's rear wheel thumped loudly as it passed over the fallen man. Im-mediately the stage began to travel faster, careening sickeningly from side to side. Shannon stuck his head out the window and looked up at the front of the coach. The driver's seat was empty and the guard's body was hanging limply over the side of the boot. Shannon could see that he was dead. The stage swerved again, this time nearly toppling over. The reason was obvious—the horses were running away, and there was no one left to pull them in. Looking down, Shannon could see the loose reins of the lead horses trailing alongside in the dirt. He holstered his Colt, took a deep breath, and threw open the coach's door.

"Don't, Clay!" Charlotte exclaimed. "You'll be killed!"

"We'll all be killed if somebody doesn't get those horses under control," Shannon replied. He grasped the frame of the door and started to swing himself up onto the roof of the coach. At that moment the stagecoach veered wildly, ran off the road, and went crashing down into a shallow gully. Shannon hung on for dear life as the stage went halfway over on its side, lost a wheel, and then slid to a shuddering halt among the rocks. The horses had broken free and were quickly disappearing into the distance.

The gyrations of the coach had thrown Shannon back into the interior. He found himself on the floor with the late Mr. Ames draped on top of him. Charlotte Alvarez was up on the seat, her small pistol in her hand. She grasped Shannon's arm and helped him struggle free of the whiskey drummer's corpse. He slumped onto the crazily slanting bench, trying to get his bearings.

"Are you all right?" Charlotte asked anxiously.

"Yes," said Shannon. "You?"

"I'm fine. Watch out—they're still firing at us!"

Two more bullets ripped through the walls of the coach, and Shannon could hear the whoops of the surviving attackers drawing nearer.

Shannon looked over at the stranger, who was resting comfortably against the windowsill and regarding him with obvious amusement.

"Mister," said Shannon, "I don't know what you think is so blasted funny, but you and I had better get outside and start shooting, or we're going to be joining Mr. Ames in Whiskey Drummer Heaven."

"After you, sir," said the stranger politely.

Shannon crawled out of the coach and crouched down beside it, looking around for the breech-clouted assassins. Even as he did so, one of them came leaping over a nearby boulder, raising his rifle to take aim at Shannon. Shannon shot him twice, and the man collapsed on the sand.

"Clay!" Charlotte cried. "Behind you!"

Shannon whirled, cocking the hammer of his six-gun. One of the attackers had appeared around the front of the coach and already had a shotgun leveled at Shannon's stomach. Shannon pulled the Colt's trigger, but the hammer fell harmlessly on an empty chamber. Shannon realized that he was standing on the edge of eternity with an empty gun in his hand. He drew back his arm to hurl the heavy weapon at his assailant, but he knew it was a futile gesture, a last act of defiance by a doomed man.

Then a pistol roared near Shannon's ear, and the painted figure jerked and fell backward, a bullet hole between his eyes. The shotgun clattered to the ground. Half-stunned by the muzzle blast of the weapon that had been fired next to his head, Shannon looked up and saw the black-clad stranger calmly returning his smoking revolver to the holster inside his coat.

"Thanks," Shannon said, a little shaken.

"My pleasure," said the stranger.

"I think there's at least two more of them out there," Shannon said, wheeling to cover the surrounding rocks.

"No," said the stranger indifferently, "they've gone." He stepped out of the coach and looked around him. "A most interesting experience," he said. "Miss Alvarez, I hope you are unhurt?"

Shannon reached up and helped Charlotte out of the tipped-over stagecoach. He looked at her apprehensively, searching for any sign of an injury. She seemed unharmed, and when she spoke her voice was quite steady.

"I don't understand this," she said. "We haven't had any trouble with Indians in this region for a long time."

Shannon holstered the Colt.

"They weren't Indians," he said.

"Not Indians?" said Charlotte Alvarez, startled. "But the breechcloths, the feathers, the war paint. . . ."

"They were white men," Shannon said. He walked over to the body of the man the stranger had shot and prodded the corpse with the toe of his boot. "Look," he said. "This is no Indian. He's dressed up like an Indian, but he isn't one. I'll wager the others weren't either."

He kicked the fallen shotgun away from the body and pointed toward a horse that stood waiting a few yards away.

"Their mounts were saddled," said Shannon. "Saddled and shod. And when was the last time you saw an Indian carrying a shotgun?"

He went over to the rock where the man he had killed had fallen and bent down over him. Charlotte came up beside him. When she saw the corpse's face, her eyes widened.

"I know this man," she said.

"Let me guess," said Shannon. "An associate of Mr. Kruger?"

"Yes. He's one of the men who stopped me in the road last week. He's the one who shot my horses."

"Take a look at that pony over there in the rocks," Shannon said. "It probably belonged to the man our friend disposed of for me a few minutes ago. See the brand on its flank?"

Charlotte shaded her eyes against the sun as she stared at the horse.

"Recognize it?"

"Yes," she said. "It's 'Box K.' That's King Kruger's brand."

"Surprise, surprise," said Shannon.

Charlotte's face flushed with anger.

"This was an ambush, wasn't it?" she said.

"Yes," Shannon replied, watching the surrounding area for signs of further trouble. "Someone knew that you were coming—or that *we* were coming—and didn't want us to reach Los Santos. Who was aware that you were arriving on this particular stage?"

"Several people," she said thoughtfully. "I wired ahead to friends to arrange for some of our *vaqueros* meet us at the stage depot and escort us out to the hacienda."

"Well," Shannon said, "it seems that one of your friends may not be so friendly after all. Or it could be that the telegrapher is too talkative, or that he's on Kruger's payroll. Anyway, it looks like Kruger got the news somehow and decided to send a few of his little playmates out to say hello."

He glanced back at the stagecoach.

"That reminds me," he said. "Excuse me, Señorita. I want a word with our fellow passenger."

He walked back to the coach where the stranger was waiting, listening without comment to their conversation.

"I want some answers, mister," Shannon said. "Just who are you?"

The stranger shrugged.

"Some call me one thing, some another. If you like, you may call me Kane."

"A little while ago you addressed Señorita Alvarez and me by name. How do you know who we are?"

Kane smiled and gazed off into the distance.

"Oh, I know a great many things," he said. "Perhaps I heard your names spoken back at the stage office in Santa Fe."

"Perhaps," said Shannon. "Perhaps not. Well, whoever you are, thanks for shooting that phony Indian off my back a few minutes ago."

"No thanks are needed. I just didn't want to see you killed before we get to Los Santos. I'm looking forward with great anticipation to your confrontation with the redoubtable Mr. Kruger. It should be most entertaining."

Shannon stared into the yellow eyes for a moment longer.

"Mr. Kane," he said, "you interest me. You seem to know as much about my affairs as I do. When we get to Los Santos, I think you and I ought to have a little talk."

He turned to Charlotte Alvarez.

"*If* we get there, that is," he said. "We seem to be in the same predicament you found yourself in last week. Afoot in the desert, with night coming on."

"It's only about ten more miles to town," Charlotte said. "We could walk it, but it might be safer to wait here. The *vaqueros* who came to meet us in Los Santos will see that the stage hasn't come in, and they'll ride up the road looking for us. I took the precaution of wiring them to do just that if we didn't arrive on time."

Shannon grinned.

"You're a very wise and prudent woman, Señorita," he said.

"I've learned from experience," she replied, opening the .32 revolver and replacing the expended cartridges. She checked the cylinder and then slipped the little weapon back inside her jacket.

"Now, gentlemen," she said, "I suggest that we make ourselves as comfortable as possible until my men arrive."

Shannon could only marvel at her coolness.

Chapter Five

T he shotgun guard's body was laid beside the stagecoach and covered with a blanket. Shannon returned
to the spot where the driver had fallen into the road,
and with Kane's assistance dragged his corpse back to
the coach and placed it under the same blanket that
was covering the guard.

"Something else Kruger has to answer for," Charlotte said, looking at the still forms.

"He's running up a big bill," Shannon said. "I'll
enjoy collecting the payment from him."

They sheltered in the shade of the wrecked coach
until sundown. Then, as darkness fell, Shannon suggested that they move back into a cluster of rocks a
few yards from the trail.

"We don't want to be too easy to find," Shannon
said. "Just in case the wrong people come calling."

They rested among the boulders, silent, lost in their

43

own thoughts. Kane sat a little distance away with his back to Charlotte and Shannon, steadfastly contemplating the rising moon.

The desert night soon grew cold, but they dared not light a fire. Shannon and the woman instinctively moved closer together, unconsciously seeking each other's warmth and companionship. It occurred to Shannon in passing that for all her strength, Charlotte Alvarez sometimes seemed slightly vulnerable and even a little lonely. He wondered vaguely if she was as lonely as he was. He quickly swept the thought from his mind, however, and they waited, together but apart, for whatever might befall them next.

Shortly after midnight, the sound of approaching horses echoed through the rocks.

"That must be our people," said Charlotte Alvarez, starting to rise.

"Or Kruger's," said Shannon. "Let's wait a moment before we go rushing out to greet them."

There were a half-dozen riders, and as they drew closer one of them saw the stagecoach lying broken beside the road, forlorn in the moonlight. He said something to his companions, and a voice called out loudly, "Señorita Alvarez! Señorita Alvarez, can you hear me?"

"It's all right," Charlotte said, getting to her feet. "That's Ramón, our foreman. Ramón! Over here! Come on, Clay. We're safe now."

Shannon followed her out of the rocks. He retrieved his gear from the stagecoach and stood patiently waiting as the *vaqueros* who now surrounded Charlotte escorted her to the waiting horses. He found himself strangely sad that their brief interval of silent companionship had ended. It was with some reluctance that he mounted the angular sorrel offered to him and set out down the road, riding a discreet distance behind Charlotte and her men.

They arrived in Los Santos just after sunup. The town was larger than Shannon had expected, although not nearly as large as Santa Fe. The appearance and the atmosphere of Los Santos were much like Santa Fe's, however, and as the first rays of the sun touched the walls of the adobe buildings, Shannon saw that this was an attractive and indeed charming place—a place well worth fighting for.

As they approached the plaza in the center of the town, they passed a large cantina. Despite the early hour, laughter and music were issuing from it. Kane pulled up in front of the door, and the others stopped and looked back at him curiously. Kane climbed down from his horse and handed the reins to one of the *vaqueros*.

"Señorita," he said to Charlotte, "traveling with you has been most amusing, but saloons are my natural habitat, and so I'll leave you now. I hope we'll meet again. And you, Mr. Shannon, no doubt I'll be seeing you again soon?"

"No doubt," said Shannon, returning the cool stare.

As Kane walked away into the cantina, Shannon felt a strange sense of relief at his departure. There was something about the man that bothered him. He had seen many gunfighters come and go—had killed some of them for that matter—and he feared no man because of his gun. Yet Kane aroused a certain wariness in him. True, Kane had saved his life during the ambush on the trail, but there was still that indefinable feeling of disquiet, a still, small voice that kept telling Shannon there was something ominous about the black-clad gambler. What was his business in Los Santos? Clearly he had come there for some purpose other than to sit in a cantina drinking or playing cards. Shannon found himself again wondering if Kane was one of Kruger's henchmen. *Well,* Shannon told himself, *I suppose I'll find out soon enough.*

The rest of the group rode on across the plaza. The fountain in the center of the square was bubbling water into a little circular basin, and Shannon found the sound soothing after the tensions of the night. At one side of the plaza stood a hotel, a pleasant-looking one-story building with a long verandah designed to shield the front of the hotel from the heat of the afternoon sun. Shannon reined up outside the entrance and dismounted. He waited while Charlotte Alvarez turned her horse and rode back to him.

"Don't leave us, Clay," she said. "We'll rest for an hour or two at the home of some family friends who live here in town. When we've refreshed ourselves and had something to eat, we'll start for the ranch. You *are* coming, aren't you?"

Shannon shook his head.

"With your permission, Señorita," he said, "I'd like to stay in town for a couple of days before I come out to the ranch. Kruger is here and the trouble is here, and I can learn a great deal more in Los Santos than I can at Rancho Alvarez. I must see for myself what we're up against. In the meantime, I strongly suggest that when you get to the hacienda you remain there, where your men can guard you from any further attack. When I've learned something more about Los Santos and about Kruger, I'll join you there. May I have the use of the horse until then?"

"Naturally you may keep the horse," Charlotte said. "But is it safe for you to remain here in town alone?"

"No," said Shannon, "it's *not* safe. But I'm used to being alone and I'm used to not being safe, and this is what I feel is best."

Concern showed in Charlotte's face.

"Be careful, Clay," she said.

"Always," said Shannon with a lightheartedness he did not feel.

"Then *hasta la vista*, Señor Marshal. I'll see you at the ranch in a day or two. In the meantime, if you need help, send word. We'll come."

"I know you will," Shannon said. "*Hasta la vista*, Señorita Alvarez."

Shannon watched as the little group of riders passed from view down a side street. After taking the Alvarez horse to a nearby livery stable, he returned to the hotel, carried his gear inside, and leaned his Winchester against the front desk. A scrawny little man in a rumpled suit came out of the hotel office and stood behind the desk, eyeing Shannon dubiously.

"I need a room," Shannon said. "One that faces on the plaza."

"You came into town with that Alvarez woman and her men, didn't you?" the clerk asked.

"Yes," said Shannon. "Why?"

"You ain't Mexican, are you?" the clerk asked suspiciously. "We don't. . . ."

Shannon stepped back from the desk and let his coat fall open, revealing the badge on his shirt.

"As it happens," he said, "I'm *not* Mexican, if that matters. My name is Clay Shannon, my ancestors came from Ireland, I'm a deputy United States marshal, I'm tired, I'm hungry, and I want a room *now*. Any other questions?"

The clerk goggled at the badge.

"I'm s-s-sorry, Marshal," he stammered. "I didn't know who you were."

He hastily removed a key from one of the pigeon-holes behind the desk and extended it to Shannon.

"Room Seven, sir. Best in the house. Good view of the plaza and the fountain."

"That should do nicely," Shannon said, taking the key.

An hour later Shannon left his room and re-entered the hotel lobby. His brow furrowed as he saw that the gambler, Kane, was sitting at a table in one corner of the lobby, playing solitaire.

Kane looked up as Shannon passed.

"We meet again, Marshal," Kane said.

"Yes," said Shannon. "What a coincidence. Are you staying here in the hotel?"

"Certainly," said Kane. "Where else would I stay?" Shannon thought he detected a hint of humor in the gambler's eyes.

"We still need to have that little talk," Shannon said. "This evening, perhaps?"

"At your convenience, sir," Kane replied. "Whenever you're ready, you'll find me in the cantina across the plaza. Until then. . . ." He nodded at Shannon and returned to his game of solitaire.

Shannon walked out of the hotel and stood on the verandah, looking around him at the plaza. Out of the corner of his eye, he noticed that a man who had been lounging against the hotel wall some yards away suddenly straightened up and hurried away across the square to a large two-story building that stood on the opposite side. The sign above the door of the building read "Los Santos Development Company, K. Kruger, Prop."

Shannon felt a sudden impulse. He was not normally an impulsive man; if he had been, he would have been dead long since. This morning, however, he was tired and irritable, with his nerves still raw from the fight in the stagecoach and the sleepless night that followed it. He wanted to take out his ill humor on someone, preferably the people responsible for the attack on the stage. Besides, he wanted to have a look at this Kruger who was causing so much grief in Los Santos, to see him and study him, so that he knew his enemy. Shannon's instinct was always to act, to confront a problem squarely and without delay. Why not, he told himself, confront this one right now?

He stepped down off the boardwalk and started across the plaza toward the Los Santos Development Company. Two men were leaning against the frame of the open front door; they watched his approach with suspicion. As Shannon neared the door, one of them pushed himself upright and moved to block the entrance.

"Whaddaya want, mister?" he said.

"I want to see Kruger," Shannon said.

"Why?"

"My business."

"Yeah? Well, you can just. . . ."

With his left hand, Shannon pulled back the lapel of his coat so that the deputy U.S. marshal's badge was in plain view. His right hand dropped to his side, near the handle of the Colt.

"I'm going in, friend," Shannon said. "You planning to stop me?"

The man scowled, then reluctantly stepped aside.

"A wise decision," Shannon said. "Which way?"

"End of the hall," the man growled, still scowling.

Shannon went down the hallway to a door marked "K. Kruger, Esquire." He pushed the door open and went in without knocking.

The office was luxuriously furnished, with rugs on the floor and paintings on the walls. The chairs were of soft leather, and a huge mahogany desk occupied one entire side of the room. Sculptures stood on pedestals in each corner, and Shannon saw that one of the busts was of Napoleon Bonaparte, another of Julius Caesar.

Behind the desk sat a heavyset man with a red face. He was wearing a white suit that was badly wrinkled, as if it had been worn for several days. Despite the luxury of the surroundings, Shannon detected a faint odor of sweat in the air.

The man in the white suit looked up in surprise as

Shannon walked in. Beside the desk stood the same individual who had been outside the hotel a few moments previously when Shannon came out of the lobby. The gunman's hand moved toward his holster as Shannon entered.

"Don't do it, sonny," Shannon said. "I'm just here for a friendly little visit."

The man in the white suit pushed back his chair and stood up.

"Well, well, well," he said with a sneer. "Whaddaya know. I'll bet you're Clay Shannon."

"And I'll bet you're King Kruger," Shannon said. "Now we *both* know."

Kruger laughed, but his eyes were wary.

"Heard you were in town, Marshal," Kruger said. "Didn't expect to see you come walking in here, though. Took some guts to do it, with all my boys hanging around. Well, now that you're here, have a seat."

"Thanks," Shannon said, still standing. "Do we have to have your hired gun gawking at us during this conversation, or can you do without him for awhile?"

Kruger jerked a thumb at the gunman.

"Get out, Snyder," he said. "I'll call you if I need you."

The man grunted and left the room.

Shannon selected one of the leather chairs and sat down. Kruger sank back into his desk chair and pulled out a cigar. He bit off the end of the cigar and spat it out on the rug. Shannon watched this performance impassively

"I'm curious," he said. "Is King a name or a title?"

Kruger guffawed.

"Right now it's my name," he replied with a broad grin. "Later on, who knows?"

"Ah, a man with ambitions," said Shannon. "How interesting."

He glanced around the room.

"Nice office you've got here," he said. "You're obviously someone who enjoys the finer things in life."

"You betcha I do," Kruger said. "And I plan to get some more of them, too."

"Like the Alvarez ranch, for instance?"

"I get whatever I want," Kruger said smugly. "No matter what it is." He lit the cheroot and blew a smoke ring at the ceiling. "Now," he said, "let's get down to business. Why have you come busting into my office so early in the morning?"

"No special reason," Shannon said. "I just wanted to see what a murderer looked like."

Kruger's face reddened.

"Don't get smart with me, Shannon," he huffed. "I know all about you. You're the fast gun from Whiskey Creek that Charlotte Alvarez thinks is going to save her hide. Well, she's got another thing coming. My men are fast guns too, the best money can buy. They ain't gonna be impressed by that tin star on your shirt, and it ain't gonna do the Alvarez family any good to try to hide behind it."

"I don't think Charlotte Alvarez is the hiding type," Shannon said. "In fact, unless I miss my guess, you're the one who ought to be doing the hiding."

"Oh, yeah? Well, I got the horses to take care of the Alvarez family, and you too for that matter. If you're smart, you'll stay out of my way. Or maybe," he said, his expression becoming crafty, "you could do yourself a bit of good by playing along with me. I got plans."

"Such as?"

"Come on, Shannon, think about it. Smart man like you ought to be able to see it right away. Before long, a few years at the most, this territory will become a state. And when that happens, land ownership will mean money and influence. Railroads will come in, and new industries that can make their shareholders rich. There'll be governors and state legislators and U.S. congressmen to elect. The people who have the power when that happens will be able to get those offices for themselves. Then they can dictate the affairs of the state, maybe even of the whole United States. You follow me?"

"Yes, I think so," Shannon said. "You want to build an empire here now, and parlay it into great wealth and political office later."

"You got it, Shannon. I knew you'd catch on."

"Big dreams, Kruger. No wonder you've got busts of Napoleon and Caesar in your office."

"Yeah, well, those guys knew how to get what they wanted. So do I. And I don't let anybody or anything stop me."

"And Rancho Alvarez is a necessary part of this fancy scheme of yours?"

"Dead right it is. The Alvarez place is the largest landholding in this part of the country. It covers nearly a hundred thousand acres. That's a huge chunk of real estate. Whoever owns it can control this entire region, and I intend to get it."

"Even if you have kill for it?"

Kruger spat noisily into a polished brass cuspidor that stood on the floor beside his desk.

"That's a stupid question," he said. "You can't make an omelette without breaking eggs. Besides, what difference does it make? These old Spanish dons are finished. New Mexico is American now, and they don't have the clout they used to. In fact, they hardly have any political pull left, except maybe with that bleeding-heart governor in Santa Fe, and he won't be around much longer. I'm gonna get them offa that land and take it for myself, one way or another. After that, the sky's the limit."

"Meanwhile," Shannon said, "you run roughshod over the people of Los Santos. Is that it?"

Kruger looked at the cigar sourly and tossed it into the spittoon.

"Can't even get a decent smoke around here," he said. "I'm gonna order me some from Cuba. Look, I do what I have to, that's all. Somebody gets in my way, I get 'em out of my way, even if I have to be a little rough about it. I take care of my friends, though. The people who stick with me will get a share of it all. That could mean big money, Shannon. Big money for you."

"I hear you've already bought the local sheriff," Shannon said, leaning back in his chair.

"Him?" Kruger said. "He's nothin'. An old drunk I made sheriff just to be sure no meddling lawman gets in my way here in Los Santos. He's the laughingstock of the town, a nobody. He's hardly worth the few dollars a month I pay him. But you're different, Shannon. You're a federal marshal. You've got a reputation, and people respect you. I could use a man like you. I'm on my way to the top. You wanta come along for the ride?"

"Sell my badge, you mean?" Shannon said.

"Sure, why not? Plenty of people do. Well, what about it? I pay much better than that Alvarez bunch. And I ain't such a bad guy when you get to know me."

Shannon stood up, eyeing him with unconcealed distaste.

"I don't sleep with rattlesnakes, Kruger," he said, "and I don't do business with cockroaches like you. No deal."

Kruger's jaw dropped.

"Why you. . . ." he spluttered, momentarily at a loss for words.

Shannon strode out of the office. As he left the building, he passed Snyder and the two gunmen who had been standing outside when he went in. A fourth man had joined them.

Shannon nodded pleasantly to them.

"Nice seeing you boys," he said. "You can go in now. I think your boss wants you."

Shannon walked slowly back across the plaza and took up a comfortable position near the door of the hotel. He knew it wouldn't take long, and it didn't. Kruger came charging out the door of the Los Santos Development Company and headed straight across the plaza toward him. The four gunmen were following, hitching up their gunbelts. They deployed themselves in front of the hotel as Kruger mounted the steps onto the verandah. Kruger planted himself directly in front of Shannon, glaring at him with his tiny, pig-like eyes.

"Mister," he said loudly, "nobody—and I mean *no-body*—walks into my office and talks to me like that."

"Oh?" said Shannon. "I thought I just did."

Kruger flushed.

"You got a smart mouth, Shannon," he snorted, "and I'm gettin' tired of it. You don't know what you're up against here, so let me give you a piece of advice—get out of Los Santos before you get hurt. It's a dangerous place for people who cross me. *Very* dangerous."

"Yes, I noticed that," said Shannon. "I especially enjoyed that little welcoming committee that met us yesterday on the road."

Kruger grinned malevolently.

"Yeah," he said, "I heard you had a little Indian trouble on the way in. Too bad."

"How did you happen to hear about it?" Shannon said. "I didn't think it had been in the local newspapers yet."

"I got eyes and ears everywhere in this town, pal. Remember that. Nothin' happens here I don't know about. And don't try to pin that business yesterday on me. I can't help what a bunch of crazy Indians do."

"At least one of the 'crazy Indians' worked for you, Kruger," Shannon said. "Señorita Alvarez recognized him. It seems he was among the brave gentlemen who helped you waylay her on the road last week. I personally made sure his horse-shooting days were over.

And another one of the 'Indians' we disposed of was riding an animal with your brand on it. Quite a coincidence, isn't it?"

The crafty look came back into Kruger's eyes.

"My brand, you say? The nag must have been stolen. Indians steal things, you know. Just like Mexicans."

"Or like fat, greedy *Anglos,*" Shannon said. "Especially ones wearing sweaty white suits."

Kruger's face became bright purple.

"I've taken all I'm goin' to take from you," he snarled. "You'd better shut your mouth before I have my boys shut it for you. All I have to do is say the word, and they'll blow you apart."

Kruger's men had been listening to the exchange. They straightened up from their careless poses, alert now, their hands hovering near their holsters. Shannon smiled pleasantly at Kruger.

"By all means say the word," Shannon said, "but if you do, I hope you don't have many plans for the rest of the day. You're standing directly between me and your hired killers, and if even one of them so much as twitches, I'll put a .45 slug in your belly before they can clear leather. Well, what do you say? I'm ready if you are."

Kruger swallowed hard.

"Don't be a fool," he said. "You can't outshoot four men. They'd get you for sure."

"Probably," Shannon said, "but by then it wouldn't make any difference to you, would it?"

Kruger glared at him for several seconds.

"Okay, Shannon," he said finally, "we'll finish this

another time. Meanwhile, I want you to deliver a message to Charlotte Alvarez and her brother for me."

"Always glad to oblige," said Shannon amiably.

"Tell them I said their time is running out. This is their last warning. They sell, or I won't be held responsible for the consequences."

"Oh, you'll be held responsible," Shannon said. "I promise you that."

Kruger gave him a look of pure loathing, then turned and went storming back across the plaza toward the building that housed the Los Santos Development Company. His men followed him, casting poisonous glances over their shoulders at Shannon as they departed.

When Kruger and his gunmen had disappeared into Kruger's office, Kane sauntered out of the hotel and leaned casually against the wall of the building.

"Bravo, Marshal," he said. "You won that round hands down. But I fear that Mr. Kruger may not let himself be bluffed the next time."

"What makes you think I was bluffing?" Shannon said.

Kane laughed.

"I can see I'm going to enjoy my stay here," he said.

"Speaking of which," said Shannon, "just exactly why are you here in Los Santos?"

"It's fate, Mr. Shannon," Kane said. "Fate has brought us together."

He laughed again and walked away across the plaza, toward the cantina.

* * *

Shannon went down the street to the little building whose sign proclaimed it to be the county sheriff's office. The door was open, and Shannon walked in.

An elderly man sat at the desk. A whiskey bottle and a glass stood on the desktop in front of him.

"Sheriff Wagner?"

"That's me, son. Hey, I guess you're that U.S. marshal they said was in town. Always glad to see a new face. Have a drink."

"Don Alejandro Alvarez was shot to death recently on the road from Los Santos to their ranch," Shannon said. "What are you doing about it?"

"Not a thing, son, not a thing."

"Why not? Isn't murder a crime in this county?"

Wagner sighed and poured himself another drink.

"Son, around here it doesn't pay to be too nosy. The last sheriff didn't understand that. The job became vacant very suddenly, while he was making his rounds one night. That's how I got to be sheriff."

"All these murders and you've done nothing?" Shannon said, his temper rising. "What kind of a law-man are you, anyway?"

"That's just it," Wagner replied. "I'm not a lawman at all. I was the town's undertaker before Mr. Kruger made me sheriff. Still am, actually. Makes it very convenient—Mr. Kruger sends a lot of business my way."

"And your deputies?"

"What deputies? I don't need any deputies. Mr. Kruger's men take care of any problems that come along."

Shannon felt revulsion creeping over him. He had nothing but contempt for any man who wore the star and didn't fulfill the obligations that came with it. He started toward the door.

"Look, son," Wagner said. "I know what you're thinking. But I'm fifty-nine years old and I mean to live to be sixty. Maybe it's different where you come from, but around here, curiosity is a luxury not many people can afford. I like this job—it's nice and quiet. I stay out of everybody's way and have plenty of time for sleeping and boozing. At my time of life, that suits me just fine. Sure you won't have a snort with me?"

"I'm sure," Shannon said, reaching for the door handle.

"Then I'll drink to your health, my boy. If you want to keep it, learn to look the other way while you're in Los Santos."

Shannon wandered about the town for awhile, carefully committing to memory the location of the various buildings and the layout of the streets. For a lawman—especially a lone lawman in a strange town—such knowledge could mean the difference between life and death.

The people he passed on the street glanced curiously at him as he went by. Most looked away quickly when they saw the marshal's badge.

Nervous bunch, Shannon thought. *Kruger must have put out the word to stay clear of me.*

Yet a few of the people he passed—all of them *Mexicanos*—smiled at him, some of the men even removing their hats politely as he went by. Apparently the Hispanic community had its own grapevine, and they had heard that he had come to Los Santos to aid the Alvarez family. *At least they know that not all Anglos are like Kruger,* he said to himself. *That's something, anyway.*

On a side street near the plaza, he came upon a mission church. He had been walking for some time, and the sun was warm. The dark interior of the church was inviting, so he entered and sat down on one of the crude wooden benches that served as pews. The place was cool and quiet, and Shannon relaxed for a moment, savoring the peacefulness and the relief from the heat.

But there was no relief from his thoughts. Nothing he had so far seen or heard had given him any reason for optimism. Los Santos was firmly under Kruger's thumb, and bringing him to justice for the murder of Charlotte's father would be difficult. Even running him out of town would be a nearly impossible task. Kruger had men, guns, and what passed for the law in Los Santos on his side. Shannon bowed his head, trying to think. What could he do? And how?

"You are troubled, my son," said a voice behind him. "Can I be of help?"

Shannon, jarred out of his reverie, leaped up and whirled to meet this unexpected threat. His hand was already on the handle of the Colt before he saw that the speaker was a priest, clad in the traditional robes of his calling.

"I'm sorry, Father," Shannon said sheepishly. "You startled me, I'm afraid. Please forgive me."

"It is I who should ask your forgiveness, my son, for intruding upon your thoughts. But I see that your reactions are very quick, and that your hand was upon your gun even as I spoke. We do not often see men of your skills here in the sanctuary."

"I'm not an outlaw, Padre," Shannon said. "My name's Shannon. I'm a deputy U.S. marshal for the territory of New Mexico."

"Yes, I see the badge now. I am Father Rosario. I was about to make a cup of *café* for myself, Señor Marshal. Will you join me?"

Shannon started to refuse, but then it occurred to him that the priest might be a useful source of information, and so he accepted the invitation.

They sat in the modest kitchen of the rectory adjoining the church. As he sipped his coffee, Shannon was sizing up the priest, trying to decide how freely he might ask the questions that crowded his mind.

"You know the Alvarez family, Father?" he said.

"Very well. Many years ago, I baptized Charlotte and her brother. Some years later, I performed the burial service for their mother. A few weeks ago I did the same for their father."

"What do you think of Charlotte Alvarez?"

"She is a fine woman, who has borne her grief with dignity and courage."

"And what do you think of King Kruger?"

"He is a vile and wicked man. But then, who among us is completely free from wickedness?"

"What do you mean?" said Shannon.

"Take yourself, Marshal. You have killed men, have you not?"

"Yes, I have," Shannon said. "When necessary."

"Then is there so much difference between yourself and men like Kruger?"

"The difference is that I kill to defend myself or others, and then only when I have to. I've sworn to uphold the law, Father, and unfortunately sometimes that's the only way to do it."

"Then you kill only to uphold the law?"

Shannon hesitated.

"No. Sometimes I've killed in anger, just as I killed the men who murdered my little boy. Does that make me vile and wicked also?"

"No, my son. But violence begets violence, and the line between good and evil can be a narrow one. Take care that you do not cross that line. Your immortal soul depends upon it."

Shannon found himself slightly disconcerted by the turn the conversation had taken. He rose and placed his cup on the table.

"Thank you for the coffee, Father," he said. "I must go now."

"I've enjoyed talking with you, Mr. Shannon. I'm sorry that my questions made you uncomfortable. I hope you'll come again—without your gun. Guns are the Devil's playthings, and I do not want them in my sanctuary."

"Guns aren't evil in themselves, Father," Shannon said. "It's the men who wear the guns, and what they do with them, that you must judge."

"I do not judge men, my son," the priest replied. "I pray for them."

"Then," Shannon said with a wistful smile, "perhaps you would be kind enough to say a prayer for me."

Chapter Six

That evening after supper, Shannon crossed the plaza to the cantina and went in. The room was large, and a number of people sat at the tables drinking or playing cards. On a platform at one side of the room, a man in Mexican attire was plucking at a guitar. Several women moved among the tables, serving the customers.

In one corner, Kane sat at a table playing cards with two other men. Shannon noted that Kane was sitting with his back to the wall, so that he could watch the door. He looked up as Shannon entered, and nodded a greeting. Then he spread his cards face-up across the table. His fellow players cursed and threw down their own hands. Disgustedly, they pushed back their chairs.

"I've had enough," one said as he rose. "Ain't no percentage in playin' poker with you, mister."

"Better luck next time, gentlemen," Kane said

smoothly, raking in his winnings. The losers headed for the bar.

Shannon went over to the table.

"You seem to have lost your pigeons," he said. "Would this be a good time for our chat?"

"Certainly, Marshal," Kane said, waving him toward a chair. "Please join me."

Shannon sat down facing Kane, watching as the gambler slowly shuffled and reshuffled the deck of cards he was holding. Shannon picked up a second deck that sat at one side of the table and glanced casually at the backs of the cards.

"At the hotel today," he said, "I asked you why you were in Los Santos. You didn't give me much of an answer, so I'll ask you again—why are you here?"

"I have my reasons," Kane replied with one of his enigmatic smiles. "Like you."

"That's still not much of an answer," Shannon said. "Look, Kane, I know a gunfighter when I see one. I've got enough trouble on my hands as it is, and I don't need more. I have the feeling that sooner or later you and I are going to get in each other's way here. I'd like to avoid that. I don't suppose you'd consider leaving town, would you?"

"No," said Kane, still smiling. "Would you?"

"No. I can't. You know I can't."

"I know," Kane sighed. "And I'm sorry. I'd regret it if you and I came to the kind of confrontation that you'll surely have with Brother Kruger. Ah, I have a suggestion. Let's play a hand of poker for it. Five card draw, loser leaves, winner stays. What do you say?"

Shannon laughed.

"Why not?" he said.

Kane shuffled the deck once more. Shannon cut, and Kane dealt the cards quickly.

"I'll take two," Shannon said, tossing his discards on the table.

"Two for the dealer," said Kane. "Tell me, Shannon, what is there in this town that's worth dying for?"

"Nothing," said Shannon. "But then, I don't plan to die here."

"Nor do I," said Kane. "What have you got?"

Shannon spread his cards out on the tabletop.

"Three aces," he said. "Looks like you're leaving Los Santos in the morning."

"Not quite," Kane said, laying down his hand. "Curiously enough, I have three aces also. Marshal Shannon, I do believe you're cheating."

"Yes, I am," said Shannon, "but only because you are. These cards are marked, and I saw the holdouts in your sleeve."

Kane laughed.

"Of course I'm cheating," he said. "I don't like to lose."

"Neither do I," said Shannon.

Kane leaped up from his chair. His right hand vanished beneath his coat and came out holding the black revolver. Surprised by the move, Shannon was a split second behind as he went for his Colt. Kane leveled his weapon and fired across the table. In the confines of the cantina, the report of the pistol was deafening.

Behind Shannon, someone screamed. His six-gun in his hand now, Shannon spun around, realizing that Kane had not fired at him. A man was lying on the floor behind Shannon's chair, staring fixedly at the ceiling. Shannon saw that it was one of the gunmen who had accompanied Kruger into the plaza earlier in the day. A drawn revolver lay beside the dead man's hand, and there was a bullet hole in the center of his forehead.

Shannon looked back at Kane in astonishment. The latter was unhurriedly returning his revolver to the holster inside his coat.

"Sorry if I startled you, Marshal," he said. "There wasn't time to call a warning. The fellow was about to shoot you in the back."

A crowd was gathering around the fallen man. There was a low grumbling, and many of the onlookers began casting hostile glances at Kane.

"Back off, you people," Shannon said loudly, displaying his badge. "I'm a deputy United States marshal, and I'll take care of this."

"Get outta the way, Marshal," one of the men said, pushing forward. "That tinhorn killed old Fred. We got a score to settle here."

"Get a rope!" somebody shouted.

The angry crowd started to converge on Shannon and Kane. Shannon had enough experience with lynch mobs to know one when he saw it. He raised his six-gun and fired a round through the ceiling. Dust rained down, and the mob hastily ceased its threatening advance.

"Back off, I said!" Shannon thundered. "The first man who lays a hand on Mr. Kane will join good old Fred on the floor there!"

He waited, six-gun poised, daring them to rush him and hoping fervently that they would not.

The ploy worked. The ring of truculent faces became sulky as their owners moved slowly away from the body and back toward the bar. Sullen glances were cast in Shannon's direction, but no one attempted any further aggressive action. The bartender came over and threw a bar towel over the dead man's face.

"Somebody go get Wagner," he said as he retreated to his place behind the bar.

Shannon holstered the Colt. Kane was sitting at the poker table, calmly shuffling the deck of cards. He appeared to be only mildly interested in the proceedings.

"Nicely done, Marshal," he said. "Very effectively handled."

Shannon sat back down at the table, moving his chair around so that he could keep an eye on the crowd.

"You didn't seem very worried about it," he said.

"No reason to be," Kane replied. "I knew you'd take care of it."

"Your faith in me is touching," said Shannon, "but what if they'd gotten past me?"

"They didn't," Kane said.

"Fortunately for you," Shannon observed dryly. "Anyhow, thanks for punching Fred's ticket for me. That's the second time you've shot someone off my back. Why are you so anxious to keep me alive?"

"I told you before—I want to see the confrontation between you and Kruger. It should be an historic occasion. It wouldn't do to have some cheap backshooter spoil the entertainment by killing you too soon."

"For the last time, Kane, why are you in Los Santos?"

"Very well," Kane said. "I'll give you one of the reasons." He gestured at the dead man lying behind Shannon. "It's because there's going to be killing here, and I enjoy watching people kill each other. Is that enough of an answer for you?"

Before Shannon could react to this startling statement, Sheriff Wagner came through the door of the cantina.

"What's going on?" he said rather plaintively.

Shannon pointed to the body on the floor.

"The character under the bar towel tried to shoot me in the back. Mr. Kane saved my life. It was a justified shooting on Mr. Kane's part, and I'll testify to that. No arrests are necessary. Anything else, Sheriff?"

Wagner hesitated, looking down at the stiffening corpse.

"Mr. Kruger ain't gonna like this," he muttered.

"He'll get over it," said Shannon. "Now why don't you run off and tell him about it? And since you're also the undertaker here, you can take that thing on the floor along with you."

"Coupla you boys carry Fred over to the funeral parlor," Wagner said. "I gotta tell Kruger."

He left, shaking his head disconsolately.

"Thanks again," Shannon said to Kane. "But if I were you, I'd think seriously about getting out of town right now. When Kruger hears about this, he may come looking for your scalp."

"I doubt it," said Kane. He started to deal himself a hand of solitaire. "Anyway, I'll take the chance."

Shannon reached into his pocket and tossed a ten-dollar gold piece on the table.

"That ought to cover Fred's funeral expenses," he said. "Seems like the least I can do under the circumstances."

Kane did not respond, so Shannon turned to leave.

"Don't forget," he said over his shoulder, "that deck you're playing with has six aces in it."

He left the cantina. Kane continued with his game of solitaire.

Chapter Seven

Shannon spent another day poking about Los Santos, talking to people and getting a feel for the town. It did not escape his notice that one or more of Kruger's men followed him everywhere he went, watching him, taking note of what he did and to whom he spoke. At length he concluded that there was little more he could accomplish there, and that he might even be placing some of the people who talked with him in danger of retaliation by Kruger's thugs.

Accordingly, the next morning he checked out of the hotel, reclaimed the borrowed horse from the livery stable, and set out for the Alvarez ranch.

The country he rode through was as parched and desolate as Charlotte Alvarez had said it was, and Shannon kept a sharp eye out for trouble. None developed, but it was with some relief that he saw Rancho Alvarez come into view.

The large, rambling house stood upon a knoll, surrounded by a high wall. A heavy iron gate guarded the only visible entrance to the grounds. Within the wall, trees and flowering bushes flourished. The place was like an oasis in the midst of the austere land around it, and Shannon wondered where the owners had found enough water to nurture so much plant life in such arid country. Predictably, the building itself was Spanish in design, even to the graceful sweep of the long verandah and the elaborate wrought-iron railings that circled the open upper galleries. The structure was elegant and imposing, and it radiated the promise of hospitality to all who entered it. Shannon urged the horse to go a little faster.

As he approached the gate, two young *vaqueros* appeared behind it, their rifles held at the ready.

"*Buenos días,* Señor," said one courteously. "I hope that you have had a pleasant journey. May I ask what business you have here?"

"Name's Shannon. Señorita Alvarez is expecting me."

The young man's face lit up with a dazzling smile.

"Señor Shannon!" he said, swinging open the gate. "I did not recognize you. But then, it's been many years since we last met. I am Carlos Rodriguez, and this is my brother, Ernesto. Your friend, Pedro Rodriguez, is our father."

Shannon dismounted, grinning with pleasure, and shook each of their hands in turn.

"I'm afraid I didn't recognize you either," he said. "Forgive me. You were much smaller when I saw you last. You've become men now, doing a man's job. Your parents must be very proud of you."

"How is our mother?" Ernesto asked. "Is our father with her in Dry Wells?"

"Yes, he's with her," Shannon said. "She's been ill, but Pedro told me before I left that she was expected to recover. He'll be coming to Los Santos to see you when he can safely leave her."

"Watch the gate, Ernesto," said Carlos, taking the reins of Shannon's horse. "Come, Señor Shannon, I will escort you to Señorita Alvarez. She will be very glad to see you."

They walked up to the house, with Carlos chatting volubly about the many pleasures of being a *vaquero* at Rancho Alvarez. As they approached the front door, Charlotte came hurrying out. She extended her hands to Shannon, a radiant smile on her face.

"Welcome, Señor Shannon," she said warmly. "Welcome to my home. It is good to see you here safe and well."

"Thank you, Señorita," Shannon said. "It's good to see you too. Los Santos is a nice town, but there's nothing there as pretty as, well, as pretty as you are." He stopped, worried that he might have offended her with his clumsy attempt at gallantry.

"Why, Marshal Shannon," she said teasingly. "I do believe you're blushing."

"I guess I am," Shannon said. "I'm not very good at compliments, I'm afraid."

"Oh, Clay," she laughed, "it was a beautiful sentiment. Thank you."

They entered the house. The room into which she

ushered him was impressive. Shannon noted with interest the fine Spanish furniture—ornate wooden pieces, dark and heavy but shining with the patina of age and quality. Family portraits and ancient tapestries adorned the whitewashed walls.

"My brother is out riding," Charlotte said. "He'll be back soon, and I'll introduce you then. In the meantime, the servants will show you to your room. Get some rest, and tonight we'll have a small dinner in honor of your arrival and in gratitude for your help."

"The honor is mine," said Shannon, feeling pleased with himself for thinking of this polite reply. "But I'm afraid I haven't done much to help as yet. I've learned a great deal in the past couple of days, but there are other things I need to know, and plans that must be made. I'll be glad when Pedro Rodriguez can come to join us. Is there any word from him?"

"Not yet," Charlotte said. "I'll have a telegram sent to Dry Wells to inquire."

"I'd rather you didn't," Shannon said. "Kruger will learn of it, and I don't want Pedro getting the kind of reception we got coming in on the stage."

That evening at dinner, Shannon found himself seated between Charlotte's aunt Carmen—an elderly woman who apparently did not hear too well—and her younger brother, Diego Alvarez, a pleasant and handsome young man of twenty or so. Diego was trying very hard to fulfill his new role as the man of the family, and drinking a little too much wine in the process.

The food was excellent, but Shannon was far from

comfortable. The conversation was largely in Spanish, and although Shannon was reasonably fluent in that language, he found it difficult to understand the accent and some of the colloquialisms used. Furthermore, he had left his six-gun in his room for fear of offending his hosts by appearing with it at dinner, and this was making him uneasy. He missed the reassuring weight of the Colt on his hip, and its absence added to his general discomfort.

However, if the Alvarez family noticed his uneasiness they hid it well, for they treated him with the same deference they might have shown to a great *hidalgo*, or even to the Territorial Governor himself. Many toasts were drunk to his coming and to the success of his mission there. This tribute, which he felt to be a little premature, made him even more uncomfortable. He was relieved when the meal was over.

The relief was short-lived, however, for as the family rose from the table, Charlotte's aunt suggested that they all adjourn to the sitting room to continue their conversation. Shannon was contemplating the prospect of another dreary hour or two of half-understood banalities when Charlotte caught his eye and gave him a conspiratorial smile.

"Aunt Carmen," she said, "I'm sure that Señor Shannon would like to see the garden. Will you excuse us while I show him around?"

Charlotte's aunt looked a little pained.

"But Charlotte," she said, "would you walk in the moonlight with a young man unaccompanied by a chaperone?"

"Don't worry, Auntie," Charlotte said. "After all,

we're Americans now, and the old Spanish customs no longer bind us. Besides, this is purely business. The Marshal and I have much to discuss regarding Señor Kruger and his gang."

"Ah!" said her aunt. "That horrible man. I only hope, Señor Shannon, that you can bring him to justice for his crimes."

Charlotte's brother clenched his fists.

"I wish I could kill him myself, right now," he said bitterly. "There is no longer any justice for people like us in this land."

Shannon rested his hand on the boy's shoulder.

"Don't do anything rash, *hermano*," he said. "Trouble will come to us soon enough—let's not invite it. You'll have your chance."

"Forgive me, Señor Shannon," said Diego Alvarez, embarrassed by his own outburst. "You're quite right. I spoke foolishly. Thank you for your wise counsel."

Charlotte led Shannon out onto the verandah and into the grounds that surrounded the house. The garden was bathed in moonlight, and Shannon noted with approval that several men with rifles were stationed along the walls. Their ominous silhouettes made a stark contrast to the softness of the night and the scent of the flowering bushes that filled the grounds.

"I'm glad to see you're taking precautions," he said. "We can't afford to be caught napping if Kruger comes to call."

"Regrettably, we have too few men left now to keep an adequate guard," Charlotte said. "Some of those *vaqueros* have been out here all night, every night, for the past week, and then doing their regular work during the day. Sooner or later they must rest."

"Then let's try to recruit more men," said Shannon. "As many as possible."

"We've tried," Charlotte said. "No one else will work for us now."

"That's unfortunate," Shannon mused. "With so few people to defend the place, a determined attack could easily gain access to the grounds. I noticed only one man guarding the front door of the house. Is the back covered?"

"Yes," Charlotte replied, "but also with only one man. There's no one else available right now. We have several riders out on the range watching over the cattle, and I've sent word for them to return at once. I'd rather not leave the range unguarded, but I suppose I have no choice."

"I'm afraid not," Shannon said. "We're going to need them here. In the meantime, we'll take whatever precautions are possible and hope that Kruger doesn't strike before we're ready for him. If he does, we'll just have to do the best we can with what we've got."

As they walked side-by-side through the garden, he recounted to her his meeting with Kruger in the plaza on the morning of their arrival. Charlotte shuddered.

"What would you have done if Kruger had ordered his men to shoot you?"

"I'd have killed him."

"But then they would have killed you."

"Possibly, but by then Kruger would be dead and your problems would be over."

"I'm not sure I'd want to pay that high a price," she said, looking up at him.

"I'd rather not have to pay it either," Shannon said. "Fortunately, we didn't have to."

"You say that the gambler, Kane, showed up after the confrontation. Do you think he would have taken a hand if there had been gunplay?"

"He might have," said Shannon, "but I don't know on whose side. He's saved my life twice now, and I suppose I should be grateful, but I still don't like the man. I've never met him before, but I know his type. He's deadly with a pistol—I've seen him shoot two men right between the eyes. Kane's a professional gunfighter, and he's not in Los Santos for his health."

"Pedro Rodriguez says you're a good judge of men and horses," Charlotte said. "Are you?"

"In my business, you have to be," Shannon replied, "if you want to stay alive."

Charlotte moved closer to him and slipped her arm through his. Shannon felt the smoothness of her skin against his hand, and it seemed to him that the night had suddenly become very warm. He wanted to draw away from her, but found that he could not bring himself to do so.

They strolled arm in arm through the garden for a time in silence.

"Tell me about your family, Clay," she said at last.

"I'd rather not talk about it, Señorita," he replied.

"Please," she said. "It sometimes helps to talk about a great sorrow. What was she like, your wife?"

"She had golden hair and blue eyes, and she was the best wife a man could ever have."

"And you loved her very much," Charlotte said, watching his face.

"Yes," said Shannon. "I did."

"She was a fortunate woman," Charlotte murmured, more to herself than to Shannon.

"She was a lot like you in some respects," Shannon continued. "She had the determination of a bulldog and the courage of a lion. I see those same qualities in you, Señorita Alvarez, if you'll permit me to say so."

"I'll permit you to say anything you like if you'll stop calling me 'Señorita Alvarez,' " she said with a musical laugh. "My name is Charlotte, as you well know."

Shannon found himself struggling to keep his mind on business. He was acutely aware of the moonlight, the perfume of the flowers, and the nearness of Charlotte's body, and he found the combination more than a little unsettling.

"It's very beautiful here in the garden," he said, trying to divert the conversation onto safer ground.

"Indeed it is," Charlotte said. "I love this house and this land. But there is evil here as well as beauty. There is also danger, especially for you. Kruger knows now that he must eliminate you if he wishes to have the ranch for himself. I fear that I've put your life at great risk, Clay. I'm sorry."

"Life is always dangerous," Shannon said, "and I'm used to evil. I've seen it often enough. I was in a church today. I met a priest there. I think he's opposed to Kruger, but I'm afraid he considers me to be a bit evil myself."

"That would be Father Rosario. He's a little naive sometimes, but he means well and the people of Los Santos hold him in high regard. I suppose I'll have to go and make my confession to him for shooting at those men who attacked us on the road the other day. Do you go to confession, Clay?"

"No," said Shannon. "If I confessed all my sins, it would take a month just to cover the major ones. I prefer to spare the clergy that burden."

"You told me you'd been a peace officer since you were very young," she said. "Where did it all begin, Clay? I'd like to know."

Shannon told her a little about his life, about being a town marshal when he was twenty, about moving from town to town, about being a lawman in raw, untamed places like Ellsworth and Wichita and Abilene and Dodge City in the heyday of the cattle drives, when the Texas men came up the trail and cared little what they did when they arrived at the Kansas railheads. He talked about how at last, weary of the constant violence, he had drifted aimlessly from place to place until finally, at the low ebb of his life, he had been offered the job as deputy sheriff in Whiskey Creek. He also told her a little about the war he waged there to save the town from the lawless men who had taken it over, and about the day his son was brutally murdered by some of those same men.

"And now Whiskey Creek is doomed," Charlotte said. "Just like your wife and boy. It must have been a bitter thing for you, watching all you valued most die before your very eyes."

"Yes, it was. It eats at you. I think it would have

eventually destroyed me. If you hadn't come to me and offered me the appointment as deputy U.S. marshal here, I doubt that I would have survived much longer. I was born to be a lawman, I guess. Anyway, I know no other way to live. I'd have been a total failure as a cattle rancher. You probably saved my life by asking for my help."

"It's comforting to hear that," she replied. "At least something good has come out of all this sadness and death."

"Only if I can save your home and your family from these men who want to take them from you. From what I've seen so far, I'm not at all sure I can do it. I warned you back in Whiskey Creek that I'm not the man you thought me to be."

"I believe you are," Charlotte said emphatically. "I've seen both your skill and your courage. You'll win this battle, Clay. I just hope you'll survive it. If I've brought you here to die. . . ."

"Don't worry about that," Shannon said. "My greatest concern is for you and your brother. You were right—Kruger's a man who'll stop at nothing, and he'll try something else, probably soon. I think we'd better start making our preparations. I suggest that. . . ."

Rifle fire shattered the stillness of the evening. It came from the front of the house, beyond their range of vision.

Shannon reached for his Colt and then remembered he had left it behind in his room. From somewhere there was the sound of glass breaking, and more shots were heard. A shrill scream pierced the night.

"That came from inside!" Charlotte cried, starting to run toward the house. Shannon caught her and pulled her back.

"Get into those bushes," he said urgently, "and stay there. They may be after you. Let me handle it."

Charlotte shook off his restraining hand.

"That's my family in there, Clay. I'm going!"

She again started for the house. Shannon cursed under his breath and hurried after her. As they ran, Shannon could hear more firing from the walls and inside the grounds. He pushed past Charlotte just as they reached the verandah. One of the Alvarez men lay moaning beside the front door. The door itself was hanging open, dangling on one iron hinge, its lock splintered by gunfire. More shots sounded inside the house, followed by another scream. Bitterly regretting the absence of his Colt, Shannon plunged through the open door into the foyer. Beyond lay the great sitting-room, and in its open doorway stood a roughly dressed man pointing a rifle into the room. Through the doorway Shannon could see Charlotte's aunt lying on the floor, blood staining the left side of her dress. Diego Alvarez was crouched over her, staring up in shock at the gunman who had shot her. The man raised his rifle again.

"So long, Alvarez," he said. "There's a hundred-dollar gold piece waiting for whoever plugs you, and I'm going to collect it."

Shannon looked around desperately. On the wall near the door hung a collection of old weapons, including several swords. He ripped one of the swords from its brackets and lunged forward. The gunman heard him coming and whirled, swinging the rifle around toward Shannon. Summoning all his strength, Shannon drove the rusty sword into the man's body. The gunman uttered a loud cry and dropped the rifle. He staggered back against the wall and then fell to the floor, writhing in pain.

Shannon tossed the sword away, then reached down and lifted the six-gun from the man's holster. He kicked the fallen rifle across the tiles toward Diego Alvarez.

"I told you you'd get your chance, Diego," he said. "Well, here it is. Stand guard over your aunt and Charlotte. Are there any more of these scum in here?"

Before Alvarez could answer, another of Kruger's men came racing up the hallway from the rear of the house, leveling a six-gun at Shannon. Shannon fired, and the man yelped in pain as he lurched to one side, clutching his left shoulder. He turned and ran back down the hall the way he had come. Shannon got off another quick shot, but the bullet buried itself harmlessly in the wall as the wounded man disappeared from view.

Shannon swore again. The revolver he had taken from the fallen gunman was old and dirty, and it lacked the easy action of Shannon's absent Colt.

Or maybe, Shannon thought, *I just plain missed him.*

More gunfire could be heard from the walls around the house, and then the sound of galloping horses came faintly to Shannon's ears. A few final shots from the guards on the walls, and then at last the night was tranquil once more.

Charlotte was kneeling beside her brother, examining her aunt's wound.

"It's bad," she said, "but it seems to have missed the vital organs. Diego, carry her upstairs to her room, and get Conchita to attend her."

Shannon hurried back out the front door, almost colliding with Ramón and two other *vaqueros*.

"Have they gone?" he said.

"*Si*, Señor," Ramón said. "They've gotten away. We don't have enough men left to go after them."

"How many of your people were hurt?"

"The man who was watching the front door was shot, but he is still alive. The two guards at the gate were overpowered. I do not know how badly they were injured."

A chill crept along Shannon's spine.

"Who were the guards?" he said.

"Carlos and Ernesto," replied Ramón. "Their father is a friend of yours, is he not?"

"Take me to them," Shannon said. "Quickly."

Ramón led him to the front gate. Carlos and Ernesto Rodriguez lay motionless on the ground beside it.

"How are they?" Shannon said to the *vaquero* who was bending over them.

"They are dead, Señor. Killed with knives. The assassins must have crept up on them in the darkness and surprised them."

Grief swept over Shannon. Pedro Rodriguez's sons were dead. Shannon had lost one son to murder; now Pedro Rodriguez had lost two.

"Oh, Pete," he whispered to the night. "I'm sorry. I'm so very, very sorry."

He grasped Ramón's arm.

"Take good care of them, will you?" he said. "Bury them properly. Their father will be here soon, and I must be able to tell him that they were treated with respect."

He walked slowly back to the house, head down, his heart heavy. Charlotte Alvarez was standing in the front hall, impassively contemplating the skewered gunman, who had now expired.

"How's your aunt?" Shannon said.

"In great pain, but I don't think the wound is fatal. One of our men has gone to bring the doctor. What will we do now, Clay?" she said.

"Fight," said Shannon.

Silently, Charlotte handed Shannon his gunbelt. She had already retrieved it from his bedroom.

"You'll need this," she said quietly.

Shannon checked the cylinder of the Colt, then returned it to its holster. He gestured at the dead man on the floor.

"Can you get one of your men to tie this carrion on the back of a horse?" he said.

"Certainly," Charlotte replied. "Where are you going?"

"Hunting," Shannon said.

Chapter Eight

Shannon rode into Los Santos the next morning with the images of the bodies of Carlos and Ernesto Rodriguez festering in his mind and fury smoldering in his heart. The packhorse bearing the corpse of the deceased gunman trailed behind, its lead rope gripped firmly in Shannon's hand.

He stopped in front of the sheriff's office and went in. Sheriff Wagner was asleep on a cot in one of the cells. He stank of whiskey.

"Come on, you, get up," said Shannon, shaking the snoring man.

"Lemme 'lone," Wagner mumbled. Shannon grabbed him by his red flannel undershirt and dragged him off the cot. He landed on the floor with a thump.

"What the . . ." he said, sitting up and peering bleary-eyed at Shannon. Shannon picked up a pail of water that was standing nearby and dumped its contents on him. Wagner gagged and scrambled to a standing position, clinging to the bars of the cell for support.

"Now wait a minute, Marshal," he said. "What's this all about, anyway?"

"A bunch of Kruger's hired guns hit the Alvarez ranch last night. They killed two men and injured another. They also shot Charlotte Alvarez's aunt. I'm going after the killers. You coming along?"

"After Kruger? Not me. I told you the other day . . ."

"Yes, you told me. You disgust me, Wagner. You're a disgrace to that badge you wear."

Wagner staggered to a chair and collapsed in it, blinking up at Shannon.

"Everything's black and white to you, isn't it?" Wagner said. "No shades of grey, no allowances for anybody's human failings. Things have to be done your way, and there's never any room for doubt, or compromise, or even mercy. Well, just wait until you're old and worn out like me, and have nothing left, not even hope."

"Or pride or integrity or guts?" Shannon asked sarcastically.

"Go away, Shannon," said Wagner with a sigh. "I've tried to warn you, but you just won't listen. You can't win here. Leave Los Santos while you still can."

"Not just yet," Shannon said.

He led the packhorse across the plaza to the walk in front of the Los Santos Development Company. Five of Kruger's men were lounging near the door. They looked as if they'd had a hard night.

Shannon halted in front of them, then reached back and cut the body loose from the packhorse. The dead man slid to the ground and lay there on his back, staring at the morning sky.

The gunmen stood gaping at Shannon with disbelief. One of them stuck his head in the door and called, "Hey, Boss, you'd better come out here."

Kruger appeared, struggling into his wrinkled white coat.

"What's going on?" he said.

"Friend of yours," Shannon said, gesturing at the body on the ground. "Thought you might like to have him back."

Kruger regarded the corpse with evident displeasure.

"You kill him?" he asked. His pig eyes were bright and mean.

"I did," said Shannon. "It couldn't have happened to a nicer guy."

"You got a lot of nerve, dumping him here like this," said one of the gunmen, bending over the body. "Look at him, Boss. They've gutted him."

The other men muttered angrily, and started to fan out on either side of Shannon, watching him with unconcealed enmity.

"No need for anybody to move," Shannon said. "Just stay put and keep your hands away from your guns, unless you want to wind up like your big bad pal there."

"What do you say he done, Marshal?" Kruger demanded.

"Well, among other brave and noble things," Shannon said, "he helped kill two boys and shot an old woman. But then, you wouldn't know anything about that, would you?"

"Not me," said Kruger. "Not my style. I wouldn't hurt a woman, or a boy either for that matter."

"Yes, you would," Shannon said. "You'd throttle your own grandmother just to get her gold teeth."

"You're pushing it, Shannon," Kruger growled, looking sideways at his gunmen.

"Let's kill this Mex-lover right now," said one of the men, fingering the butt of his revolver.

"My friend," said Shannon icily, "if you open that filthy mouth of yours again, I'm going to take that six-gun you're playing with and shove it down your throat. Now, I don't suppose any of you would like to tell me where you were last night, would you?"

"We ain't tellin' you nuthin'," said another of the gunmen, a man named Finch. "You can't prove a thing on us."

"No?" said Shannon. "Where's your other hired killer, Kruger—the one with the bullet wound in his left shoulder? I'll bet I can prove something against *him*."

"Ain't none of *us* got any bullet wounds," said a third man. "You'd better take that tin badge and get out of here before we decide to put a few bullets in *you*."

Shannon leaned forward in the saddle, resting on the saddle horn.

"I notice that some of you boys have dried mud on your boots," he said. "Not much mud around here in the dry season. About the only place you'd find wet ground anywhere nearby would be at the Alvarez ranch, in the garden where they irrigate the plants. The earth there is about that same color too."

"You're crazy," said a small man with a ferret-like face. "We ain't been nowhere all night. We was playing poker until dawn right here. Ain't that so, boys?"

Shannon was studying the ferret-faced man's belt. He dismounted and stepped up on the boardwalk, then walked over to the little man and stood in front of him, his face hard.

"One of the people I'm looking for is pretty handy with a knife," he said. "Now, that's a nice-looking one you've got there in your belt, friend. You want to let me see it?"

"I'll let you see it between your ribs, law dog," snarled the man. He whipped the knife out of its sheath and lunged at Shannon. Shannon's Colt was in his hand before the man had moved a half-step. He swung the barrel of the six-gun hard against the man's head, dropping him to his knees. The knife skidded onto the sidewalk in front of him and he knelt there dazed, holding his head and moaning. Shannon bent over and picked up the fallen knife. There were dried bloodstains on the blade.

"You little monster," Shannon said, "you're a real terror when it comes to killing boys in the dark, but you're not quite so tough when you're face to face with a grown man in the daylight."

"Lester there havin' a knife don't prove nothin'," Kruger said. "Plenty of people carry knives around here."

"Do they all have fresh blood on them?"

"He skinned a jackrabbit last night," said Finch. "We ate it for dinner, right boys?"

"See?" Kruger said. "You ain't got a thing on any of us. We're clean."

"Kruger," said Shannon, "you're a liar, a thief, a murderer, and a back-shooting coward. I'm going to see to it that you answer for everything you've done—everything, including last night at the Alvarez ranch."

Kruger's features twisted in rage.

"That's it, Shannon," he yelled. "I've had all I'm gonna take from you. *Get him, boys!*"

Gunhands twitched, but Shannon's Colt was already covering the four remaining men. Three of them decided not to chance it, but one was less cautious. He cursed and went for his holster. Shannon shot him. The gunman fell backward through the window behind him, landing on the floor inside the building in a welter of broken glass.

Instinctively, the other three men started to draw their weapons. Shannon waited for them, the hammer of his six-gun cocked and ready.

"Go ahead," Shannon said. He knew it was insane to take on three professional gunslingers alone, but the pent-up anger he had controlled for so long was now surging up in him, completely overwhelming his reason. "Go ahead," he said again, his voice cracking with emotion. "Pull 'em. I wish you would. *I really wish you would.*"

The men slowly eased their six-guns back into their holsters.

Shannon wheeled and centered the muzzle of the Colt on Kruger's abdomen, his anger now at the boiling point. Kruger saw death in Shannon's face, and thrust his open hands out before him to show Shannon they were empty.

"Don't shoot!" he cried. "Don't shoot! I ain't even got a gun!"

Shannon felt his finger tightening on the trigger. He had never shot an unarmed man, but he thought again of Pedro Rodriguez's dead sons, butchered like animals by Kruger's men, and knew that this time he was going to do it. Kruger realized it too, and he let out a squeal of fear.

"Hold it, Marshal!" said a voice behind Shannon. "Uncock that Colt and slide it back into the holster."

Shannon recognized the voice immediately. It was Kane.

"About time you showed up, Kane," Kruger fumed. "You took long enough. What do you think I'm paying you for, anyway?"

"The Colt, Shannon," Kane said. "Put it away. I've got a .45 aimed right at your spine."

Shannon hesitated, weighing his chances, but he quickly concluded that it was no use. He had seen Kane's skill with a gun, and he knew the gunfighter wouldn't miss him, not at that distance. Shannon let the six-gun slip back into its holster, then turned his head to stare at Kane.

"At last you have your answer," Kane said. "Surprised?"

"No," Shannon said, "I'm not surprised. Just disappointed."

"Drill him, Kane!" Kruger bawled. He was still shaking with fright.

"I don't shoot people from behind, Kruger," Kane said. "I don't like backshooters."

"Yeah," Kruger grumbled, "so you told me last night after you plugged Harris in the cantina. Well, I didn't hire you to kill *my* people. I hired you to kill *their* people, and that includes this two-bit lawman. Now let him have it."

"My, my," said Kane mockingly. "You must think Marshal Shannon is a very dangerous man."

"You better believe he's dangerous. He just proved it by blowing one of my people through my own office window. That's why I want you to shoot him."

"Not a smart move, Kruger," Kane said. "Look around—we've attracted quite a crowd here, and it wouldn't be healthy to gun down a U.S. marshal in broad daylight in front of three dozen witnesses, not even in this town. They've all heard you tell me to kill Shannon. You sure you want to risk it?"

Kruger glanced around the street. The gunfighter was right—a sizeable group of onlookers, attracted by the shooting, were watching the proceedings intently.

"They wouldn't dare talk," Kruger grumbled. "I got these people buffaloed."

"The locals, maybe," Kane said. "But who else is in that crowd? A traveling salesman, perhaps, or someone else just passing through. Maybe even a prominent citizen from another town, someone who might get attention if he talked. You couldn't be sure the word wouldn't get out, and then you'd have all sorts of problems. Those political connections you like to brag about wouldn't care for that kind of publicity. They'd turn on you in a minute. No, I think we'll have to save Mr. Shannon for another day."

"Well . . ." Kruger said grudgingly. "Okay, Shannon, that crowd's saved your neck for the moment, but there'll be another time, a time when there ain't any witnesses. Then you'd better look out."

"Now that we've settled that, Kruger," Shannon said, "collect your sorry pack of rats and get out of my sight. Take your knife-happy friend along too— there's no point in me arresting him, because if I put him in jail, that tame sheriff of yours would turn him loose as soon as I went out the door. Speaking of which, don't forget to have Mr. Sheriff-and-Part-Time-Undertaker Wagner haul away that dead meat that's lying on the floor of your office."

"Okay, boys," Kruger said reluctantly, glaring at Shannon. "It's a standoff. Pick up Lester and let's go."

"I'll be seeing you, law dog," the ferret-faced man hissed as he climbed to his feet, still holding his bleeding head.

"Yes," said Shannon. "You will. And all of you remember this—with or without Kane backing you, if any of you try to draw on me again—today, tomorrow, next week, or ever—you'll just be saving the hangman some trouble, because I'll take out this Colt and turn you into buzzard-bait. Now, is that clear enough for your tiny little minds to grasp, or do you want me to explain it again?"

The gunmen glowered at Shannon and began to retreat slowly back into the building. Kruger started to follow them, then paused and looked around at Shannon. His eyes were red with hate.

"You're a walking corpse, Shannon," he said. "You'll never leave Los Santos alive."

"So everybody keeps telling me," said Shannon. "Now crawl back into your hole. And remember this— if I don't leave here alive, neither will you. I guarantee it."

After Kruger and his men had re-entered the building and slammed the door behind them, Shannon turned to face Kane. The latter's six-gun had again disappeared inside his coat. The crowd began to disperse, sensing that the show was over.

"Kane," Shannon said, "if you keep saving my life, Kruger's going to ask for his money back. Why didn't you shoot me? Or let them do it? You certainly don't care about witnesses—not you, not in Los Santos. That was just an excuse. Your boss told you to finish me off. Why didn't you?"

"Kruger's a swine," said Kane. "I want to see if you can get him before he gets you."

"You're a strange one," Shannon said. "You've saved my life three times now, even though Kruger's hired you to kill me. But if you stick with Kruger, you know that sooner or later you and I will have to have it out between us. I wish I could persuade you to leave town before that happens."

"Sorry," Kane said. "I've taken Kruger's money, and I'll do what he's paid me to do. I never welsh on a contract or double-cross a patron. It's a point of honor with me. Besides, it would be bad for business. Now go on your way before one of Kruger's men bushwhacks you through that broken window. And the next time we meet, don't count on me being so generous."

Baffled by it all, Shannon walked away, wondering as he went if Kane would change his mind and shoot him in the back before he was out of range. But no bullet came, and when Shannon looked around again, Kane was nowhere in sight.

Chapter Nine

Shannon stood on the balcony of the ranch house with Charlotte Alvarez by his side. They were watching the sun sink slowly toward the distant hills. The sunset was spectacular in its beauty, but Shannon hardly noticed. His mind was on other things.

"So you were right about Kane all along," Charlotte said.

"Yes," Shannon replied morosely. "I wish I hadn't been."

"But why would Kruger attack the stagecoach carrying his own man?"

"My guess is that Kruger didn't know Kane would be on that particular stage."

"This Kane—will you have to fight him, Clay?"

"Undoubtedly."

"Will you win?" Charlotte asked. Had Shannon

been less preoccupied, he might have noticed the tremor in her voice.

"I don't know," he said. "Kane's as good with a gun as any man I've ever seen."

"As good as you are?"

"I'd say so. Maybe better. I suppose we'll find out eventually. Right now, however, I'm only thinking of one thing—how I'm going to tell Pedro Rodriguez that the two sons who were his pride and joy are dead, killed while I was a few yards away, walking in the garden."

"He won't blame you."

"I wish I could be sure of that," Shannon said. "I know what it's like to lose a son. It can crush you, make you bitter and vengeful, poison your life."

"Is that what it did to you?"

"I suppose so—for a while, at least. I think I've gotten past all that now, but it wasn't easy. I'm just sorry Pedro has to go through the same thing."

"Pedro's tough. You've seen that yourself, back in Whiskey Creek. Like you, he'll go on, no matter how deep his grief."

"I hope so," said Shannon. "I wonder when he's coming."

He came the next day, in the afternoon. He rode up to the gate of the ranch house on his own horse, leading Shannon's buckskin.

While the servants put away the horses, Shannon and Charlotte welcomed Rodriguez as best they could, making small talk as they escorted him into the house. They asked about his wife, Maria, and were told that she had recovered from her illness. Rodriguez was visibly tired by the long ride from Dry Wells, but Shannon knew that they could not postpone the breaking of the news about his sons any longer. They took him into the garden, out of sight of prying eyes, sat down with him on one of the benches, and told him as gently as possible what had happened. Tears ran down Charlotte's cheeks as Shannon recounted the attack that had cost Carlos and Ernesto Rodriguez their lives.

When Shannon had finished, Pedro sat there for several minutes, staring blindly at the flowers. His eyes remained dry, but his face was a mask of pain as the reality of it sank in. Shannon's heart nearly broke as he watched his friend come to grips with the fact that he would never see his beloved boys again.

At last Rodriguez raised his head.

"Maria must be told," he said in a strained voice.

"I'll send a man into Los Santos to the telegraph office in the morning," Charlotte said. "Write out the message you want to send her."

"Thank you, Señorita," replied Rodriguez. "That is very kind of you."

He fell silent again for a time, then spoke again.

"Where are they buried?" he asked in a husky voice.

"We laid them to rest in the cemetery just beyond the walls, out there underneath the trees," Charlotte said. "It's been the burial place of my family for generations. We thought it only fitting that since your sons died defending us, they should share our resting place. I hope you approve."

"You are very kind," Rodriguez said. "It is a great honor. May I have a minute or two with them?"

They took him out to the cemetery that lay on the next rise from the house. It was a pretty spot. Shannon and Charlotte waited a little distance away, watching as Rodriguez stood with bowed head, alone for the last time with his two sons. *If Kane outdraws me, I wonder if they'll bury me here too?* Shannon thought. *I guess it's as good a place as any. But it's a long way from those two graves in Whiskey Creek.*

When they returned to the house, Pedro stopped in the hallway and looked searchingly at Shannon and Charlotte Alvarez.

"I know both of you well enough to know that you are blaming yourselves for the deaths of Carlos and Ernesto," he said. "Do not do so. They were doing what they wanted to do, serving your family, Señorita Alvarez, as their grandfather and their great-grandfather did. You bear no responsibility for what happened to them. It is the evil men who killed them who are guilty. I ask only that we act soon to bring the murderers to justice. I want vengeance, and I will have it—one way or another."

Pedro asked to be excused, and with Charlotte's ready permission he retired to the Alvarez family's little chapel to light a candle for the souls of his dead children. Charlotte went to attend her injured aunt, promising to return as soon as possible.

Shannon was glad to have the brief period of solitude, for he had a great deal to think about. Despite the sadness of the reunion, he was pleased that Pedro Rodriguez was with him again. There had been a time when he preferred to fight his wars alone, depending on no one, but now, after all these years, he found it comforting to have help. Perhaps it was because he was getting older, or because he had fought so many battles and was growing tired of fighting. Or perhaps it was just that he was depressed by the odds against him.

And the odds were formidable. Kruger had Los Santos in his pocket, and could do what he liked there. It was a safe haven from which he could operate without fear of consequences. And he had many men working for him—at least a dozen, perhaps more. Shannon had already eliminated some of them, and ironically Kruger's own gunfighter, Kane, had helped the cause by killing several others. But trying to shoot down all of Kruger's hired guns was hardly a solution, even if it were possible. No matter how many were killed or frightened off, Kruger could always get more. The West was full of footloose gunmen who would gladly work for him. Shannon was badly outnumbered, and would continue to be.

In addition, Kruger had complete control of the local law. This in itself was crippling Shannon. Wherever he went, even a deputy U.S. marshal, with all his authority and jurisdiction, needed the support of the city marshal or county sheriff to accomplish his mission. But the pathetic puppet Kruger had installed in the Los Santos sheriff's office was powerless to oppose Kruger's actions even if he had wanted to, which clearly he did not.

Further, it was apparent that, at present at least, Shannon could expect no help from the people of Los Santos. Even the ones who detested Kruger would be afraid to take any action against him, because of his hired gunmen and his vicious tactics. Kruger ruled Los Santos, and no one who lived there dared challenge him.

And perhaps worst of all, time was against Shannon. If Charlotte and Diego Alvarez did not surrender their land to Kruger soon, he would surely try again to kill them. Since at Shannon's insistence both brother and sister now reluctantly remained secluded at Rancho Alvarez, never venturing into town, Kruger's only means of getting at them would be to attack the ranch house again. Because of the unexpected resistance offered by Shannon and the Alvarez *vaqueros*, the first attempt had been defeated. Next time they would be better prepared, and come in greater force.

But what to do about it? The house would be hard to defend against a determined assault. The walls that enclosed the grounds were high, but the surrounding terrain was higher. Several hills overlooked the house. Men hidden on them would be able to see over the walls and take the defenders under fire, subjecting them to a virtual siege if Kruger wished. However, Shannon doubted that a man like Kruger would have the patience for that. It was more likely that he would order his men to launch a direct assault, attempting to storm the hacienda by naked force either by day or by night. The attack could come at any time, and its chances of success would be high.

Therefore, to protect Rancho Alvarez and save Charlotte and Diego from being murdered, there was only one choice—Shannon must go on the offensive, taking the fight into Los Santos itself, confronting

Kruger on his own ground. But how? Shannon wandered through the garden alone, pondering the problem.

Presently Charlotte joined him there, and they sat on one of the benches under the trees, sheltered from the afternoon sun. Shannon told her of his conclusions, and his fears for her safety. Charlotte remained silent for a moment, considering what he had just said.

"Why is Kruger doing all this, Clay?" she asked. "I still don't understand that."

"I think I do, now," Shannon said. "Kruger told me himself. Actually, you guessed the reason for it when you and I first met in Whiskey Creek. Kruger lusts for power. It's just that simple. And you're in his way, you and your family and your land."

"But why must he have Rancho Alvarez? Why are we so important to him?"

"Charlotte," Shannon said gently, "this ranch is the key to everything he wants. He knows possession of it will bring him the power he craves."

"Yes, but this is dry, sparsely populated country, remote from Santa Fe and the other large towns. We actually occupy and use only a small fraction of what we own. The land won't support any more cattle than we're presently running here, and in any event the days when there was a great fortune to be made in beef are gone. How does taking over our ranch bring him power?"

"Because of its vast size," Shannon said. "It covers a good portion of this part of the territory, as you know. And whatever else Kruger is, he's a shrewd man who's foreseen the future. The old Southwest, the

Southwest your family has known for so long, is changing rapidly. Statehood is coming, and with it vast wealth and influence—for those who control the land. Land like this. The wealth and influence that the land brings will mean votes, and Kruger has political ambitions. He wants to be governor or a senator or whatever else he can grab."

"Somehow, I can't see a thug like Kruger in the governor's mansion," Charlotte said. "The man must be mad."

"He is mad," Shannon said. "Power-mad. He's a classic case, a cheap, small-time hoodlum who has a dream, or perhaps I should say a twisted vision, of building an empire for himself. He's in the right place at the right time, and knows it. He sees an opportunity here, an opportunity he can seize only if he can take over Los Santos and the territory around it. To do that he must drive away the present landowners, the old Spanish families who ruled here before the annexation by the United States of the New Mexico Territory, families like yours. So he preaches hatred against the *Mexicanos* and terrorizes the people of Los Santos with his brutality to make sure they won't dare oppose him. As for the landholders, he drives out those he can and kills the rest. That's why your father is dead, Charlotte. He stood between Kruger and Kruger's demented dreams of empire, and he paid for it with his life."

Dinner was a silent affair. Charlotte's aunt was not present; she was recovering nicely from her wound, but would not be able to leave her bed for many days.

Charlotte, young Diego Alvarez, and Pedro Rodriguez sat at the table with Shannon, while Shannon recounted to Pedro all that had happened, and the difficulties they faced.

"Tell me one thing, Clay," Rodriguez said. "Do you know which of Kruger's men killed my sons?"

"I think it was a little reptile named Lester. He has a reputation with a knife, and there was blood on the blade the next morning in Los Santos when I knocked him down and took the knife from him. Unfortunately, I have no proof against him."

"Perhaps in time we shall find the proof," Rodriguez said. "And when we do . . ." He left the sentence unfinished.

"Meanwhile," Shannon said, "We have our work cut out for us."

"Indeed we do," said Rodriguez. "Truly, this Kruger and his gang are terrible men, and they have us at a great disadvantage. So, *amigo*, how do we defeat them?"

"As I see it," Shannon said, "the first step is to get the backing of the people of Los Santos. Without their support, we'll have little chance of accomplishing anything."

"If that is what is needed," Pedro Rodriguez said, "that is what we shall do. You have a plan?"

"Yes. Feel like taking a little tour of the town with me tomorrow?"

"It will be a pleasure, *amigo*. What time do we start?"

Chapter Ten

Shannon and Pedro Rodriguez left the house at dawn. Charlotte argued hotly that she should come with them because of her knowledge of Los Santos and its people.

"No," Shannon said firmly. "When Kruger finds out we're in town, there may be trouble, and I don't want you getting hurt."

"I can help, Clay."

"Yes, you can—by staying here with Diego. Keep the *vaqueros* at the house today also. When Kruger learns that Pedro and I have left, he might be tempted to try something against you. I'm betting he'll be too preoccupied with us in Los Santos to strike here, but there's no way of knowing that for certain. Do you have any binoculars?"

"I do," said Diego. "They were my father's."

"Then use them to keep checking the high ground

beyond the walls. If Kruger's men are watching the place, we need to know it. All right?"

"Very good, Señor Shannon," Diego said. "We will do as you say."

"Good luck, Clay," Charlotte said. "Come back safely. I—we—need you."

This time Shannon noted the quiver in her voice.

"I'll come back," he said.

"I'll be very upset if you don't," said Charlotte with a sad smile. "*Very* upset."

"I wonder what she meant by that?" Shannon said to Rodriguez as they rode away.

Rodriguez laughed.

"My friend," he said, "I believe that the lady of Rancho Alvarez has become somewhat attached to you. Why I cannot imagine, but if you don't come back to her as she asks, you are indeed a very foolish man. She is a lot of woman, that one. The face of an angel and the heart of a tiger. And surely you have seen the way she looks at you."

"I hadn't noticed," said Shannon truthfully. It had never occurred to him that the growing attraction he felt for Charlotte Alvarez might be mutual.

They rode into Los Santos, watchful and well aware that they were alone in enemy territory.

"Let's talk to the priest, Father Rosario, first," Shannon said. "He's not particularly fond of me, but he has great prestige among the people, and maybe we can persuade him to use it. Just don't shoot anybody when he's around—he doesn't care much for guns."

They found Father Rosario on his knees before the altar, praying.

"May we talk to you, Father?" Shannon said, when the priest arose.

"Let us go outside," Father Rosario said, eyeing the leather gunbelts and blue steel six-guns that Shannon and Pedro Rodriguez were wearing. "As you know, I do not like to have firearms in the sanctuary."

They found a shady spot on a bench in the cloister behind the church, and accepted Father Rosario's invitation to sit down. Shannon introduced Pedro Rodriguez to him. The priest looked thoughtfully at the badge on Pedro's shirt.

"Another man of the law, I see," he said. "It is strange to find so many of you in a town that both law and justice have forgotten. Well, my sons, what can I do for you?"

"Father, we want to end King Kruger's reign of terror in Los Santos."

"Kill him, I suppose you mean?"

"No. We want to arrest him and make him stand trial for his crimes."

"That is something I would very much like to see. But what can I do?"

"We want to hold a meeting of the townspeople, Father. We want to bring together everyone in Los Santos who is against Kruger, and ask for their support."

"Why do you need it?" said the priest. "You are lawmen. It is you who should enforce the law."

"Lawmen can't enforce the law by themselves," Shannon replied. "They must have the backing of the people. That's the only way the law can be upheld anywhere—with the support of the people the law is meant to protect. And it's the only way that Kruger and men like him can be defeated."

"I see. I hadn't thought about it like that. You are right, I suppose, Marshal Shannon. But few would come to such a meeting, I think. They are all too wary of Kruger. They'd fear retaliation."

"As isolated individuals they're reluctant to act," said Shannon. "It's only human to hesitate to resist tyranny when you're alone. But there's strength in numbers, and courage as well. If we can bring the people together, show them that they're not alone, that there are others, many others, who are willing to stand shoulder to shoulder with them against Kruger, they may find that their courage has returned, and decide to help us to help them."

"And you hope to accomplish all that with this meeting?" said the priest. "I doubt that it would work, and in any case such a gathering would be certain to bring Kruger and his men down upon us. There would be violence, gunplay, bloodshed. No, gentlemen, I know you mean well, but I will not help you."

"You have violence and gunplay and bloodshed in Los Santos now," Pedro Rodriguez said. "That is what we wish to put an end to."

"Violence begets violence," said the priest.

"It sometimes prevents more of it," Shannon said. "Look, Father, we're willing to risk our lives to help the people of this community. Surely you're willing to do the same?"

Father Rosario sighed.

"You are very persuasive, Mr. Shannon," he said. "Exactly what is it that you wish me to do?"

"Spread the word among the people of Los Santos about the meeting. Use your influence to get them to come. And come yourself."

"And where is this meeting to be held?"

"Where else?" Shannon said, pointing at the church.

"I never thought he'd go along with it," Pedro said as he and Shannon left the mission half an hour later. "Well done, *amigo*."

"He agreed to let us hold the meeting in the church," Shannon said, "but it's clear that he thinks very few will come. We've got to find some way to encourage people to attend."

"What do you suggest?"

"I think we ought to try to speak to this man Ricardo Morales that Charlotte told us about," Shannon said. "Apparently his family and hers have been friends for many years. She stopped at their home when we first arrived from Santa Fe. He's what might be called a 'leading citizen' here—or at least he used to be before Kruger came. Let's see if we can get his support."

They found the Morales home easily. It was a large house on a shaded lot near the edge of town. Although not as impressive as the Alvarez home, it was obviously the residence of a well-to-do family.

A servant girl opened the door in response to their knock.

"We'd like to see Señor Morales, please," Shannon said. "My name's Shannon. I'm a deputy United States marshal. I believe Señorita Charlotte Alvarez may have mentioned me to Señor Morales."

"Please wait, Señores," said the girl. "I will see if Don Ricardo is at home."

She closed the door again.

"Unusual to keep visitors standing outside in the heat," Rodriguez said. "Spanish hospitality is usually a little warmer than that." He removed his hat and wiped his brow with a handkerchief. "Not that it isn't quite warm enough out here," he added.

"I don't think it's a lack of hospitality," Shannon said. "Did you see that girl's expression when she opened the door? She was just plain scared."

"More of Kruger's handiwork, no doubt," said Rodriguez.

Presently the door opened again. This time the girl was smiling.

"Please come in, Señores," she said. "Don Ricardo will see you in the library."

She ushered them down a short hall and into a pleasant room with windows that looked out onto a small garden. The walls of the room were lined with books, and a volume of poetry lay open on a low table beside a comfortable-looking chair.

An elderly man entered the room, removing a pair of spectacles as he did so.

"*Buenos días,* Señores," he said, placing the eyeglasses carefully on the table beside the open book. "Señor Shannon, Charlotte told me of you when she visited us a few days ago on her way back to Rancho Alvarez. Welcome to my home. Please be seated. I regret that you were kept standing outside in the sun.

Señor Kruger and his friends have made us all cautious of strangers, I'm afraid."

"That's what we want to talk to you about, Don Ricardo," said Shannon. "You know why we're here in Los Santos, and we need your help." He told Morales of the planned meeting that evening at the church, and explained the purpose of it.

"Your reasons for attempting to hold such a meeting are quite sound," Morales said. "Unfortunately, I fear that your effort will be unsuccessful. The people of Los Santos will not risk antagonizing Kruger."

"That's just the point, Don Ricardo," Shannon said. "We must persuade them to take the risk in order to save themselves from Kruger and his crowd. I can see that you're an intelligent and well-educated man, and Charlotte Alvarez tells me that you're held in great esteem here. If you urge your fellow citizens to attend the meeting, at least some of them will come. What's more, if you would come to the meeting yourself, many others would take heart and follow your lead. Can we count on your support?"

Morales gave a wan smile.

"No, Señor, I regret that you cannot," he said. Shannon started to protest, but Morales held up his hand to stop him. "Let me explain why I feel as I do, so that perhaps you will not think quite so badly of me," Morales said. "I too have tried to oppose Kruger, to arouse the good people of Los Santos against him, just as you are trying to do now. I found it to be not only impracticable but unwise."

"But surely Kruger wouldn't try his strong-arm tactics on *you*," Shannon said.

"Would he not?" Morales replied. "I have a young granddaughter, Mr. Shannon. She is ten years old, and she lives with Señora Morales and me because her parents are dead. She is a lovely child, and the light of my life. Within hours after Charlotte Alvarez left the house the other day, someone pinned a note to my front door with a knife. The note was addressed to me, and it stated that if I ever again spoke up against Kruger, or aided anyone who did, my granddaughter would be killed. Since then I have said and done nothing further regarding Kruger, nor will I do so now."

Shannon was silent for a few seconds, trying to think of an appropriate response.

"Señor," he said, "Marshal Rodriguez and I have come here to rid Los Santos of Kruger once and for all. We can't do that unless the people will back us. All of the people, including you."

Don Ricardo wearily rubbed his eyes.

"I realize that, Marshal Shannon. But I believe this devil Kruger would do exactly what he says he will do. He's done such things before to those who have opposed him. As you may have heard, scarcely three weeks ago a man who had urged resistance to Kruger was found dead, hanged in the plaza. There is nothing of which Kruger is not capable, no act of violence that is too extreme for him. I am not afraid for myself, but I will not risk my granddaughter's life. Furthermore, I am, in effect, no longer a citizen of Los Santos. My wife and I are taking our granddaughter and leaving for Mexico in a few days. We will not return. In the meantime, I will undertake no action that might induce Kruger to carry out his threats."

"If we could offer you the protection of the law," Shannon said, "would you stand up with us against Kruger?"

"There is no law in Los Santos now," Morales replied. "That is precisely why we are leaving. You are brave men, Señores, and please believe me when I say that I appreciate very much what you are trying to do. But could you assure me that there would be no danger, that my family would not be harmed, if I were to do as you ask? I think not."

"That's true," said Shannon reluctantly. "I can't eliminate the risk inherent in this meeting, nor can I guarantee that no harm will result to those who come. But unless the people of Los Santos, including prominent men like you, are willing to take the risks involved and fight back against Kruger, it's unlikely that the town will ever be free of him. Marshal Rodriguez and I will try, of course. We'll fight Kruger alone if necessary, but we're only two against many, and the odds are very much against us."

He stood up.

"Thank you for seeing us, Don Ricardo," he said respectfully. "I'm sorry to have troubled you."

When they had been shown out of the house, Shannon and Rodriguez began to walk back toward the plaza.

"Do you think he will change his mind?" Rodriguez asked.

"Not unless something changes it for him," Shannon said. "And Kruger's got this town so thoroughly intimidated, I really don't know what that something might be."

"Then what now, *amigo*?"

"I think the attitude of everyone in Los Santos is affected by the fact that the sheriff is Kruger's man," Shannon mused. "If we could alter that, if the people knew that the local law no longer belonged to Kruger, it might give them the courage they need."

"And how could we cause such a change?" said Rodriguez.

"I don't know," Shannon said. "But let's head for the sheriff's office. I want you to meet the good Sheriff Wagner, and I want to talk with him to see if I can help him find *his* courage. If he has any."

As they approached the plaza, Rodriguez glanced over his shoulder.

"You are aware, are you not," he said, "that two men are following us?"

"Yes," said Shannon. "I spotted them a few minutes ago. They're Kruger's people. If Mr. Kruger doesn't know we're in town yet, he soon will."

They reached the sheriff's office and entered it. The two trailing gunmen took up positions where they could watch the door.

Wagner was sitting at his desk, whittling on a piece of wood.

"Well, well," he said, "the great man himself. I figured you'd be dead by now, Shannon. Who's your friend? Ah—I detect another badge. Not a federal one, though, I see."

"This is Pedro Rodriguez. He's the marshal of a town up north called Dry Wells."

"I've heard of it," Wagner said. "Bit out of your

territory, aren't you Rodriguez? Well, what do you gentlemen want from me?"

"We want you to help us get Kruger."

Wagner's jaw dropped in surprise.

"You're crazy, Shannon," he said, sitting upright in his chair, "or you else you think I am. I told you before—I'm not a real lawman. I'm just the local undertaker."

"No you're not," Shannon said. "You're the sheriff of Los Santos. That star on your chest says so. And because you're the sheriff, you have an obligation to the people of this town, an obligation to defend them from men like Kruger. For heaven's sake, man, don't you care about what he's done to this community?"

Wagner ran his hand over his face.

"Of course I care," he said. "I may be old and tired and useless, but I haven't forgotten the difference between right and wrong. It's just that there's nothing I can do about it. I'm no gunman. If I tried to shoot it out with Kruger's men, they'd kill me for sure."

"We're not asking you to shoot it out with them," Shannon said. "All we're asking you to do is come with us to the mission tonight and tell the people of Los Santos to join together and oppose Kruger. If the town turns against him, and you put the weight of the sheriff's office behind us, Marshal Rodriguez and I will take care of the rest."

"What 'weight of the sheriff's office?' " Wagner said with a bitter laugh. "Everybody in town knows I'm just a no-good drunk with Kruger's brand stamped on my backside."

"Then get up on your hind legs and show them

they're wrong about you. Show them you're a man, a lawman, and you're not anybody's flunky anymore. Take back the respect you've lost. Show the people of Los Santos you're on their side, not Kruger's. You carry the star. Act like it."

"You want me to come to this meeting and speak out against Kruger?"

"Yes."

Wagner shook his head.

"Sorry, I won't do it. I can't do it. I'm . . . well, the truth is, I'm afraid. Haven't you ever been afraid, Shannon?"

"Everybody's afraid sometimes. What counts is going ahead despite the fear and doing what needs to be done."

Wagner rested his elbows on the desk, put his head in his hands, and closed his eyes.

"It's no use," he said. "You're wasting your time on me. Twenty years ago, ten even, I might have had the sand to do what you're asking. It's too late now. I can't help you."

Shannon watched the sagging shoulders and the lowered head momentarily, then turned away.

"Come on, Pedro," he said. "This isn't a man, it's a mouse. Kruger's mouse. Goodbye, Wagner. I feel sorry for you."

"I do too, son," Wagner said in a low voice as Shannon closed the door behind him.

Shannon and Rodriguez moved back up the street toward the plaza. One of the two gunmen continued to follow them. The other had disappeared.

"Gone to tell Kruger where we've been, I suppose," Shannon said.

They had not eaten since early morning, so they stopped at a café. The other people in the establishment watched them nervously as they ate. Some got up and left without finishing their food.

"Looks like Kruger has these people so edgy they don't even want to sit in the same room with us," Shannon mused. "Gives you a warm feeling, doesn't it?"

"They may have good reason for avoiding us," Pedro said. "It is never wise to linger in the vicinity of an obvious target. One could be struck by a stray bullet."

When they came out of the cafe again, the same man was still following them.

"I don't know about you," Shannon said to Rodriguez, "but I'm tired of being tailed. Let's have a word with that clown."

They reversed course and moved back toward the gunman who had been shadowing them. The man stopped short when he saw the two lawmen approaching. Several passersby paused also, sensing that something was about to happen.

"My friend," Shannon said to the gunman, "I don't like being followed. This is the last time I want to see you today. Go away. Fast. Otherwise I'll arrest you for vagrancy, premeditated obnoxiousness, and aggravated criminal stupidity. Understand?"

The man hooked his thumbs in his gunbelt and sneered.

"What'll you do after you arrest me, Shannon? You

ain't even got a jail to put me in. You gonna take me all the way to Santa Fe on those phony charges?"

"That's a problem, I admit," Shannon said. "But then, if I had a jail to put you in, you and your friends would already be in it. As it is, I guess I'll have to think of something else."

"Yeah? Like what? You gonna shoot me?" He gestured at the watching bystanders. "Look, all you people," he called. "I ain't touched my gun. The Marshal ain't got no cause to draw on me."

"Shooting you isn't necessary," Shannon said. "At least not this time." He stepped forward, jerked the man's revolver out of its holster, and tossed the weapon out into the street. Then he took the gunman by the seat of the pants and heaved him bodily into a nearby horse trough. Water slopped out onto the ground as the man sat up in the trough, coughing and spitting.

"What'd you do that for?" he spluttered.

"You needed a bath, and I needed the exercise," Shannon replied. "Now go back and explain to Kruger how you got all wet, and then tell him I said the next man I have to throw into a horse trough won't sit up like you're doing. He'll be too busy trying to breathe, because I'm going to hold his head underwater until he stops kicking. Got it?"

"You're the one who's going to get it, Shannon," the man said, climbing out of the trough. Water ran from his clothes onto the ground. The spectators were grinning broadly, and he glared malevolently at them.

"Get outta here," he shouted. "This ain't none of

your affair." The grins disappeared, and the spectators hurried away, eyes averted.

"Move out, mister," Shannon said to the gunman. "And don't forget to tell Kruger what I said."

The man started into the street to pick up his revolver.

"Never mind the six-gun," Shannon said to him. "I'll leave it in the horse trough for you."

"That was worth seeing," said Rodriguez when the gunman had gone.

"I'd rather have shot him," Shannon said dryly. "But making him a laughingstock like that is even better. The people who saw what happened will talk about it to others. Jokes will be made about it. If the humor will lessen people's fear of Kruger even slightly, it may increase the attendance at our meeting tonight."

A small boy came running up to them.

"You're Marshal Shannon, ain'tcha?" he asked. "My ma told me to come find you. She just took some of Sheriff Wagner's laundry into his office, and she says to come quick because he's hurt."

Shannon and Rodriguez exchanged looks, then hurried after the boy back to the sheriff's office. A woman holding a bundle of clothing was standing on the walk outside the office. She looked upset.

"He's in there," she said, pointing at the open door. "I didn't know what to do."

Wagner was lying on the floor of the office, groaning. His face was a mass of bruises, and blood was trickling from his nose and mouth. Shannon pulled him up and helped him to the bunk that stood against one wall of the office. As he lay down on the bunk he cried out and clutched at his side.

"What happened, Wagner?" Shannon asked. It was an unnecessary question, for he had already guessed the answer.

"Kruger's men," Wagner said through swollen lips. "Broke in through the back door. Beat me. Kept hitting me, kicking me. Thought they'd never stop. I begged 'em, but they wouldn't stop. Said if I went to that meeting of yours, they'd kill me."

"Someone must have been eavesdropping while we were talking with you," Shannon said. "I'm sorry, Wagner. I didn't expect this."

Wagner pulled out a soiled bandana from his pocket and dabbed at his face. Shannon took the cloth from him, soaked it in some water from a pitcher that stood on a table behind the desk, and began to wipe away the blood.

"Broken nose," Shannon said. "Couple of teeth missing, too. They worked you over pretty thoroughly. How many were there?"

"Three, four, I don't know. They came at me so fast, I never even saw 'em 'til they'd already grabbed me."

"Recognize any of them?"

"Sure. Snyder, Lester, and Finch. Red Harper was there too, I think. The others were hitting me so hard I couldn't tell for sure."

"Pedro," Shannon said, "if that kid's mother is still waiting outside, ask her to get a doctor, will you?"

"I don't need a doctor," Wagner said. "I've been

beaten up before. I wish I hadn't begged them, though. They shouldn't have made me beg."

"Take it easy, Sheriff," Rodriguez told him. "Rest awhile. Is there anybody we can get to come and stay with you?"

"I don't have anybody," Wagner said. "Thanks anyway."

"Come on, Pedro," said Shannon. "We've got some work to do. Wagner, I'm really sorry about this."

"It's okay, Marshal," Wagner said. "Serves me right, I guess."

Shannon and Rodriguez started for the door. Wagner sat up on the bunk, pressing his hand against his ribs, and called to them.

"Marshal?" he said. "What time is that meeting tonight?"

"Eight o'clock. Why?"

"I'll be there," Wagner said. "You can count on it—now. They shouldn't have made me beg. They should never have made me beg."

Shannon came out of the sheriff's office and started toward the plaza. Pedro Rodriguez walked beside him.

"You are going after the men who attacked the sheriff?" said Rodriguez.

"We can't just let it pass," Shannon said. "If we want the office of sheriff to mean anything in Los Santos, the men who assaulted Wagner will have to pay for it."

They rounded the corner into the plaza and headed for the Los Santos Development Company. As usual, a few of Kruger's gunhands were lounging outside the door.

"That tall one's Snyder," Shannon said. "I don't see Lester or Finch or Harper."

The gunmen shifted their weight nervously as the two lawmen approached.

"Snyder," Shannon said, "give me that gun. You and I are going to have a little talk."

"Nobody takes my gun," Snyder said. "Besides, I ain't done nothin'."

"Yes, you have," Shannon said. "You've irritated me, and that isn't nice." Before anyone could react, Shannon reached over and seized Snyder's six-gun. He handed the weapon to Rodriguez.

"Hold that will you, Pete?" Shannon said. "And keep an eye on the rest of these sidewinders. I'll be back in a few minutes."

"Take your time," said Rodriguez. "These gentlemen and I will wait, won't we boys?" He drew his own revolver and covered the remaining gunmen.

"Start walking," Shannon said to Snyder, pointing up the street.

"Where?" Snyder said. He looked worried.

"How about Kruger's livery stable?" Shannon said. "I'm sure you know where it is."

"Why're we goin' there?"

"We're going to talk about horses. Move."

Reluctantly, Snyder preceded Shannon along the street to the livery stable. The sign painted on the wall beside the stable door said "Los Santos Livery, K. Kruger, Prop."

"Inside," Shannon said. Snyder went in, glancing apprehensively back at Shannon.

When they were inside, Shannon closed the doors and bolted them.

"What's goin' on?" Snyder said. His voice was shrill.

"Who else besides you beat up Sheriff Wagner?" Shannon said.

"I dunno what you're talkin' about," Snyder mumbled.

Shannon cocked the six-gun in his hand. Snyder tried to back away, but was brought up short by the boards of the stall behind him.

"Answer the question, please," Shannon said.

"Okay, okay," Snyder said. "It was me and Lester and Finch."

"What about Red Harper?"

"That lily-livered worm?" Snyder said scornfully. "He was too soft-hearted to help. Tried to get us to stop. We'll take care of him later."

"So it was you and Lester and Finch who attacked the sheriff?"

"I already told you that."

"On Kruger's orders, I assume?"

"Yeah, he said Wagner needed a lesson."

"An excellent precedent," Shannon said.

"Aw, come on," Snyder grumbled. "I didn't even hit the old fool. I just held him."

"You held him while the others hit him?"

"Well, yeah."

"What did you do when he begged you to stop hurting him?"

"Huh? Just held him. Kruger said to give him a good goin' over."

"So you held him while the others hit and kicked him and he begged you for mercy?"

"Yeah. What's the difference? He's just an old drunk."

Shannon slipped the Colt back into his holster. He unbuckled his gunbelt and hung it on a peg beside the door.

"He's the Sheriff of Los Santos, Snyder," Shannon said. "He wears the star, just like I do. Let's see if you can do to me what you did to him."

Snyder glanced at Shannon's gunbelt hanging on the peg, and grinned.

"You're gonna be sorry you did that, Shannon," he said. "I'll whip you good."

He lunged at Shannon. Shannon sidestepped and drove his right fist into the side of Snyder's head. Snyder sprawled onto the floor, stunned.

"You're not doing very well so far," Shannon said. "Could it be that you're only good at beating up old men?"

Snyder let out a roar and came at Shannon, trying to grapple with him. Shannon sank a left into the gunman's stomach and followed with a right to his jaw. Snyder went over backwards into a pile of hay bales.

"Let me help you up," Shannon said. "You seem to have trouble staying vertical today." He took Snyder's arm and started to lift him to his feet. Snyder cursed and shook free, then came at Shannon again, swinging wildly. Shannon drew back his arm and hit Snyder full in the face. Snyder went head over heels, crashing against the side of an empty stall. The boards broke, and Snyder cartwheeled into the stall, sliding through the dirty straw. Shannon stepped forward and waited for him to regain his feet.

"Get up," Shannon said. "We're not through with our discussion yet."

But Snyder had no intention of getting up.

"No more, Shannon!" he sniveled. "No more! I had enough. Don't hit me again."

Shannon went over to the door and took the gunbelt off the peg. He strapped it back on, watching with disdain as Snyder groveled in the muck of the stall.

"You miserable hyena," Shannon said, "if you ever touch Wagner again, we'll have another session like this. And next time I won't hear you when you ask me to stop. You might want to pass that thought along to your friends Lester and Finch, because it goes for them too."

He opened the doors and went back up the street.

Pedro Rodriguez was still waiting in front of the Los Santos Development Company. He was idly fingering his six-gun and smiling benevolently at the three Kruger gunhands who were backed against the building's wall.

"So soon?" Rodriguez said as Shannon approached. "Too bad. The boys and I were having such a nice time."

"Where's Snyder?" one of the gunmen asked.

"He'll be along in a minute," Shannon said. "If he can crawl this far."

"Have we any other business with these good fellows?" Rodriguez asked Shannon.

"Not at the moment," Shannon said. "We may want to resume the conversation at a future date."

"Then we shall leave you now," Rodriguez said to the Kruger men. "I suggest that you do not try to shoot us in the back while we're walking away. It would be most ill-advised. In fact, it would probably be fatal—for you. Good day, *gentlemen*."

Chapter Eleven

A few minutes before eight o'clock, Shannon, Rodriguez, and Charlotte and Diego Alvarez arrived at the mission. Shannon was nervous and unhappy. He had not wanted Charlotte and Diego to come.

"It's too dangerous," he had said. "You'd be playing right into Kruger's hands. Stay at the ranch. It's safer."

But Charlotte had been adamant, and Diego had followed her lead.

"I can be useful, Marshal," he said. "My family name is well respected among the people of Los Santos. I will speak to them, urge them to do as you wish. It might make the difference between success and failure for you."

"But . . ." said Shannon. Charlotte touched a finger to his lips, silencing him.

"We will go," she said. Her voice was quiet, but

the steel was there again. Shannon knew immediately that arguing with her would be pointless.

He did at least persuade Charlotte to bring along four of her *vaqueros* to act as a bodyguard. He would rather not have weakened the defenses of the hacienda by taking the men into town with them, but Charlotte's safety—and Diego's of course—were the first priority. He gave the men their instructions, and the group set out for Los Santos. Shannon rode silently, disturbed that Charlotte and Diego were going into the lion's den with so little protection. If Kruger wanted to kill them, he'd never have a better chance.

At the mission, they found Father Rosario waiting at the door.

"How many, Father?" Shannon asked.

"More than I expected," the priest answered. "It seems that many of them heard about the way you humiliated Kruger's man on the street today. You made him look ridiculous. The people are laughing about it, and laughter can be a powerful weapon. More powerful even than a gun."

Sheriff Wagner arrived, limping and holding his side.

"How bad is it?" Shannon asked him.

"Not too good," Wagner said. "Busted ribs, I guess. But I'm here. You got your wish, Shannon. I'm going to be a sheriff now."

The church was nearly full. Most of those who had come were *Mexicanos*; some were *Anglos*. All of them were men. This did not surprise Shannon, for he knew that no sane man would willingly bring a wife or child to such a gathering. The danger was too great. The surprise was that so many people had come at all. The waiting men had been talking with each other in hushed tones; as Shannon and the others entered, the talking stopped, and all eyes were turned upon them.

The priest began by introducing Shannon and Pedro Rodriguez. There was no need to introduce the two members of the Alvarez family, for they were well-known to everyone in Los Santos. Then Father Rosario spoke to the group at length, urging them to listen to Shannon and the rest. Shannon talked to them briefly, repeating many of the things he had said earlier to the priest and the other people he had spoken to.

"But Señor Shannon, what will happen to us if we stand up to Kruger?" one of the men asked.

"What's going to happen to you if you don't?" Shannon replied.

"Can you promise us that Kruger will not do something to us or our families if we help you?" another man said.

"No," said Shannon, "I can't. You know that. There's danger in this, certainly, but you must ask yourselves if it's any more dangerous to act than not to act. You must ask yourselves if you're willing to let Kruger continue to rule this town. You must ask yourselves if you're willing to pay the price for being free men again."

The debate went on. Diego Alvarez stood up and spoke.

"You all knew my father," he said. "He was a great man, and a great friend to the people of Los Santos.

Many of you worked for him at one time or another. I speak to you tonight in his place, and I say to you the words he would have said. Kruger must be stopped. Marshal Shannon and Marshal Rodriguez have come to help us, but we have to help ourselves as well. Now. . . ."

He spoke of his father, and what his father would have done; he spoke of good and evil, and pointed out which one Kruger represented. Then he went on to talk about duty, and pride, and honor. Shannon was astonished by his eloquence. Truly, the son was stepping into his father's shoes, assuming the role that Alejandro Alvarez might have played if he were still alive.

"Just listen to him!" Charlotte murmured to Shannon as Diego spoke. "It's amazing! He's not a boy any longer, Clay. My little brother has grown up."

"I'm proud of him," said Shannon. "Of you, too. But I still wish you hadn't come. Kruger isn't going to be pleased when he finds out how many people are here tonight. Odds are there'll be trouble before the evening's over."

"I don't care if there's trouble," Charlotte said. "I'm not going to hide in my home while you and Diego and the others risk your lives." There was passion in her voice as she spoke, and fire in her eyes. Shannon again found himself admiring her courage as well as her beauty. He decided that Charlotte Alvarez was indeed, as Pedro Rodriguez had put it, a lot of woman.

The debate went on. Shannon left the sanctuary and joined Rodriguez outside on the church steps, where the latter was standing guard. He had posted two of the Alvarez riders at the front of the church, and two more in the cloister behind it.

"We'd all better stay awake," Shannon said. "If Kruger's going to make a play, he'll do it soon. I wish we had more men."

"I notice that Señor Morales did not come," Rodriguez said. "A pity."

"Yes," said Shannon ruefully. "His presence would have meant a lot. I don't blame him, though. He's concerned for his granddaughter, and rightly so. Considering some of the other things Kruger's done, he probably wouldn't have any qualms about harming a ten-year-old girl."

"Look," Rodriguez said, pointing. "Someone's coming."

Shannon peered in the direction indicated. The full moon illuminated the street, making the two approaching figures clearly visible.

"Is that Kruger?" Rodriguez asked. "The fat *hombre* in the white suit?"

"In person," Shannon said. "And that's Kane with him."

Shannon and Rodriguez reached simultaneously for their holsters, slipping the rawhide loops off the hammers of their six-guns.

"Alert the men," Shannon said.

"No need," said Rodriguez. "They've already noticed. Hold your fire, *muchachos*. Don't shoot unless they shoot first. What do you think, *amigo?* Will there be gunplay?"

"I wish I knew," said Shannon, hefting the Colt to make sure it was loose in the holster. "I hope not, especially not with Charlotte and all the others in the church. Well, we knew the risks when we decided to do this. Now we'll just have to wait and see what those two vultures want."

Kruger came up the steps like a runaway train. Kane followed at a more leisurely pace. Even in the moonlight, Shannon could see the wrath on Kruger's red face.

"Shannon, just what do you think you're doing?" he rasped.

"Good evening, Mr. Kruger," Shannon said mildly. "What seems to be the problem?"

"You're the problem, Shannon. You and this meeting. What are you trying to do, stir these people up against me?"

"Yes," said Shannon.

"Well, you can stop right now," Kruger barked. "I've spent a lot of time and effort teaching these morons not to mess with me, and I ain't gonna let you spoil it now. I want this little pow-wow broken up, savvy? Tell them all to go home and stay there, or I'll do it for you. Never mind, I *will* do it for you. Outta my way. I'm going in there and boot them all out."

"Sorry," Shannon said. "Admittance by invitation only. And you're not on the guest list."

Krueger's face was now purple.

"How're you gonna stop me?" he demanded belligerently.

"Oh, I'll think of something," Shannon replied. "By the way, I notice you didn't bring your usual collection of hoodlums along with you tonight. Where are they? Out beating up women and children?"

"They're around, Shannon, they're around. And anyway, I don't need them. Kane here can take you anytime. Right now, if I tell him to."

"That's not very bright, Kruger," Shannon said. "Ask Kane. He knows I'll get you before he gets me."

Kruger could only glower at Shannon in frustration.

"I'll see you again," he said angrily. "Soon. Real soon."

"I'll look forward to that," Shannon said. "Don't stay away too long."

Kruger snorted something unintelligible and stamped away, mouthing curses beneath his breath. Kane remained behind on the church steps.

"Don't underestimate him, Shannon," Kane said. "Just because he's a loudmouthed bully doesn't mean he's not dangerous. You know that by now. I promise you that what he just said was no idle threat. I don't tell tales out of school, but he'll try to get back at you for what you've done. And like he said, it'll be soon. He's already set it up."

"Thanks for warning me," Shannon said. "That's another one I owe you."

"Don't get me wrong," said Kane. "This doesn't change anything between us. Sooner or later you and I are going to have a showdown, if Kruger doesn't get you first."

He turned and followed his employer into the night.

Inside the church, Sheriff Wagner was now addressing the crowd.

"You've got to stand up to Kruger, folks," he was saying. "I've learned that."

"Yeah, Ed," someone called, "you stood up to him,

and look what it got you. I don't want Kruger's people breaking my face and kicking in my ribs."

There was a murmur of agreement from the crowd. Shannon could see that they were not persuaded by what had been said to them. They were getting restive, and would walk out of the meeting soon if something was not done to convince them. He moved to the front of the church and spoke to Father Rosario.

"Father," he said, "the other day when we sat in your kitchen I noticed a pile of dry sticks next to the wood stove. I assume you use them for kindling when you light a cooking fire. Can you get me about a dozen of them? I'll also need a piece of twine."

The priest looked at him uncomprehendingly.

"But why?"

"Please, Father, can you get them?"

The priest hurried off, returning in a few seconds with an armload of the sticks and a length of heavy string.

Shannon put the sticks and the string on a bench and held up his hand to get the attention of the group.

"There's an old fable I want to remind you of," he said. "Would one of you assist me?"

"This is no time for stories, Marshal," said someone in the back. "We've been here too long already."

"It won't take but a moment," Shannon said. He handed one of the sticks to a man in the first row.

"Can you break this?" he said.

"What?" said the man, puzzled. "Break it? Sure."

He snapped the stick in two and tossed the pieces on the floor in front of Shannon. Shannon picked up the remaining sticks and wound the twine about them, tying them securely into a single bundle. He handed the bundle to the man who had broken the single stick.

"Can you break *this*?" he said.

The man took the bundle and strained to break it in half.

"I . . . I can't do it," he puffed, after several seconds of trying.

"Exactly," said Shannon, taking back the bundle and holding it up so that all could see. "One stick alone is weak and easy to break. Many sticks bound together can't be broken, no matter how hard someone tries. Do you understand now? Alone you're at Kruger's mercy, but acting together you're strong, unbreakable. Think about it."

The men on the benches stared silently at the cluster of sticks in Shannon's hand. Shannon handed the sticks to Father Rosario and walked out of the church. Charlotte followed him.

"I remember that old story now, Clay," she said. "How did you happen to think of it?"

"Desperation," Shannon said, "People are usually more impressed by what they see than by what they hear. They may not have been persuaded by our words, but they'll remember the sticks."

The men who had attended the meeting began filing out of the church. They said little, but they seemed thoughtful.

Pedro Rodriguez was still standing on the steps.

"Any sign of trouble?" Shannon said.

"Nothing," Rodriguez replied. "Everything's quiet."

"Too quiet," Shannon said. "Let's get started back to the ranch before Kruger does something nasty."

Diego Alvarez came out of the church.

"Did I do well, Marshal?" he asked. "I tried to say the things my father would have said. Do you think it helped?"

"I know it did, *hermano*," said Shannon. "Well done!"

Diego beamed.

One of the *vaqueros* brought up the horses. They mounted and swung their mounts' heads around to start out of town, with two of the *vaqueros* in the lead and Shannon bringing up the rear, watching for any sign of pursuit.

"Keep a sharp lookout," he warned the others. "We don't want. . . ."

The street was lit by a flash from a gun muzzle, and the report echoed sharply between the buildings. A *vaquero* grunted in pain and fell to the ground. More shots followed, the sound filling the night. Diego Alvarez went down as his horse bolted away. Shannon kicked the buckskin and charged at the gun flashes, firing his Colt.

"Pedro!" he shouted over his shoulder. "Stay with Charlotte!"

Several of their party were firing back. The bullets whipped past Shannon as he rode into the line of fire. Behind him Pedro Rodriguez was calling to the *vaqueros* to stop shooting so they would not hit Shannon, and then Shannon was at the mouth of the alley from which the gunshots had come. Through the gloom he could make out dark shapes running away up the alley—two men, each carrying a rifle. He caught glimpses of their silhouettes as they fled through the patches of lamplight that shone from the windows of the adjacent buildings. Shannon urged the buckskin after the fugitives. He thumbed off two more rapid shots, but the light was uncertain and the chances of hitting a running man from the back of a running horse were slim.

The Colt was empty now, and Shannon had no time to reload. He pulled his rifle out of its saddle scabbard just as he caught up to the closest man. He swung the barrel of the Winchester hard against the back of the man's head as the buckskin galloped past him. The man sprawled on the ground and lay still. Shannon was almost at the end of the alley now, and he hauled the buckskin to a stop just as another muzzle flash told him that the second man was right ahead of him, a few yards from the dead end. Shannon sent the buckskin leaping forward again and barreled into the gunman. The man let out a screech of fear and pain as the horse crashed into him. He went down, and his rifle bounced away into the shadows. The buckskin stumbled as its hooves thudded into the falling body, then regained its balance just as Shannon brought it to a halt and swung out of the saddle. He cocked the Winchester and ran back the half-dozen yards to the spot where his horse had collided with the second man.

In the square of yellow light cast by a lamp in a nearby window, Shannon saw a form lying on the ground. He ran up, rifle at the ready.

"Help me!" the fallen man whined. "My leg's busted!"

"Good," said Shannon, standing over him.

Just in time Shannon saw the muzzle of the six-gun swinging up toward him. He twisted to one side as the man pulled the trigger, and the bullet tugged at the fold of his shirt, burning his skin as it went past. He fired twice into the downed man's shadow, and a scream followed by a gurgle told him that he had hit his target at least once. Cautiously he again bent over the gunman's body. The man was dead, his heart pierced by Shannon's bullets.

Shannon ran back up the alley to the spot where the first man had gone down. Just as he came upon the prostrate figure, two of the *vaqueros* led by Pedro Rodriguez rode their horses into the alley, coming full at him.

"Hold it, Pedro!" Shannon called. "I've got them!"

Someone said something in Spanish, and Rodriguez shouted "Don't shoot! It's Marshal Shannon!"

As they dismounted and ran toward him, Shannon bent over the first gunman's slumped form.

"One of Kruger's men, naturally," Shannon said, trying to catch his breath.

"Is he alive?" Rodriguez said, coming up beside him.

"No," said Shannon, uncocking the Winchester. "Too bad. There are a few questions I would have liked to ask him."

"And you, my friend—you are all right?" Rodriguez asked anxiously.

"Yes. You?"

"Sí."

"Charlotte?"

"She wasn't hit. You'd better come back, though. Diego's hurt. I do not know how serious it is."

Shannon retrieved his horse and hurried back into the street where the ambush had occurred. Three of the *vaqueros* had dismounted and were crouched, rifles at the ready, looking around for further danger. The fourth *vaquero* was lying between them, trying to get up. He moaned and collapsed as Shannon approached. A few feet away, Charlotte Alvarez was kneeling in the street, holding Diego in her arms and weeping.

"Get some light out here," Shannon snapped. "Hurry."

Even as he said it, someone ran up carrying an oil lamp and lifted it high. In the lamp's yellow glow, Shannon saw that Diego was shot through the body. Blood covered his shirt.

Shannon went to his knees beside him.

"Señor Shannon," Diego gasped, reaching out for him. "I can't move my legs." Shannon gripped the boy's hand. It was as cold as ice.

"Marshal," Diego said, "I *did* do well tonight, didn't I?"

"You did splendidly, Diego," Shannon said. "Your father would have been proud of you."

"Charlotte?" whispered Diego, trying to look up at Charlotte. "Charlotte, are you there? I can't see you. Please don't leave me."

"I won't leave you, Diego," Charlotte said through her tears. "I'm right here."

The boy smiled, gazing up at her. Then his eyes glazed and the labored breathing stopped.

"Oh no," Charlotte said fearfully. "Oh, Clay, is he . . ."

Shannon was feeling for a pulse. There was none.

"He's gone," Shannon said. He released Diego's limp hand and knelt there, his head bowed, hearing only Charlotte's sobs as she cradled her dead brother's body to her.

The injured *vaquero* had pulled himself painfully along the ground toward them.

"Don Diego!" he called. "Don Diego!"

"He can't hear you, Manuel," Shannon said.

"Madre de Dios!" the *vaquero* cried. "He cannot be dead! Señorita Alvarez, I'm so sorry. I wish it had been me. It should have been me. Forgive me! Forgive me!"

Charlotte gently eased Diego's lolling head down to the earth.

"It's all right, Manuel," she said. "You did all you could. I'm glad you survived. Lie back now, and we'll get you some help."

Someone was pushing through the crowd that encircled them. He was carrying a medical bag.

"Get out of the way," the man said. "I'm a doctor." He knelt beside Diego.

"Never mind, Doctor," Charlotte said in a tired voice. "There's nothing you can do for Diego now. Please see to Manuel—he's badly hurt."

Shannon stood up. Pedro Rodriguez was beside him.

"Clay," he said, "there must have been a third man in the alley. There are blood spots leading out of the alley and away up the street."

"I only saw two of them," Shannon said. "The other one must have gotten away before we went in there. It's curious, though—only two rifles were firing at us."

"We'd better get Charlotte out of here," said Rodriguez. "They may try again."

"Yes," Shannon said. "Take her back to Rancho Alvarez. Hurry."

"What about you?" said Rodriguez.

"I'll be along in a few minutes," Shannon replied. "First there's something I have to do."

"Wait," said Rodriguez. "I'll go with you."

"No, I want you to stay with Charlotte. See that she gets home safely. When you reach the hacienda, put all the *vaqueros* out on guard in case Kruger's people come after her there."

"Where will you be?" Rodriguez asked.

"Killing rats," Shannon said.

He strode rapidly up the street toward the plaza, reloading his rifle and six-gun as he went. The offices of the Los Santos Development Company were locked and dark. Shannon kicked open the front door and went in.

"Kruger!" he called. "Kruger, where are you?"

He went down the hall and tried to open the door of Kruger's office. It too was locked. Shannon raised the Winchester and fired. The bullet smashed the latch, and the door swung open. The office was dark and empty.

Someone came up behind him in the doorway. Shannon swiveled around, rifle at the ready.

"Easy, Shannon," said a voice. "It's me, Ed Wagner."

"Where's Kruger?" Shannon said.

"I dunno," said Wagner. "He's not here, that's for sure. A couple of people out there in the plaza told me he closed up the place and went off down the street before the shooting started. Going under cover until the fireworks were over, I guess. He could be any-where. You'll never catch up with him."

"Yes I will," Shannon said. "Find a lamp and light it."

Wagner went into the office and groped about for a few seconds. Then he struck a match, and an oil lamp flared. Shannon briefly checked the room to make sure that Kruger was not hiding somewhere in it.

"This is Kruger's office, you know," Wagner said. "He won't like you coming in here."

"Kruger just tried to kill me," Shannon replied. "What he does or doesn't like really doesn't interest me much anymore."

He looked around the office at the expensive fur-niture, the rug, the paintings, and the sculptures of Bonaparte and Caesar. Then he handed his rifle to Wagner.

"Here," he said. "Hold this for me."

He picked up one of the heavy chairs and swung it with all his strength against the desk. The chair splin-tered. Taking one of the broken chair legs, Shannon methodically began to destroy the office, shattering the marble busts, knocking the paintings off the walls, fracturing the desktop. Next he went around the room smashing the glass out of the windows.

"Give me the lamp," he said.

Wagner handed it to him.

"Go on outside," said Shannon, taking back the Winchester.

Wagner started to object, then changed his mind as he saw the look on Shannon's face. He hurried back down the hallway and out the front door. Shannon hurled the lamp against the desk. It broke, sending oil splattering across the floor. Flames from the burning wick quickly set the carpet alight.

Shannon took one final look around, then walked unhurriedly out of the building.

A crowd had gathered.

"The building's on fire!" someone yelled. "Get the fire brigade!"

"I'll shoot the first man who tries to put it out," Shannon said. There was no more talk of calling the fire brigade.

One of the Alvarez *vaqueros* was there, holding the buckskin's reins.

"I have your horse, Señor Marshal," he said.

Shannon took the reins from him, mounted the buckskin, and rode out of town, the *vaquero* following. As they passed out of Los Santos, Shannon looked back. The red glow of flames lit the sky. Shannon kicked up the horse and rode away. He did not look back again.

Chapter Twelve

They buried Diego Alvarez the next morning in his family cemetery. Father Rosario performed the rites, with Charlotte at the graveside. Shannon stood back a little way, watching.

When the service was over, Shannon walked slowly back toward the house with Charlotte. She had not wept at the cemetery, but the grief on her face was plain for anyone to see. It cut through Shannon like a knife.

"I failed you, Charlotte," Shannon said disconsolately. "I failed to unite the people of Los Santos against Kruger, and I got Diego killed. I've brought you only pain."

Charlotte put away her rosary and took Shannon's arm.

"Clay," she said, "you've fought bravely and you've

145

done your best. No one could ask more. There are just some things even you can't overcome."

"Maybe," said Shannon. "But this isn't finished yet. I'll avenge Diego for you if it's the last thing I ever do."

"Please don't risk your life again, Clay," she said. "Vengeance won't bring Diego or my father back. There's been enough killing already. I don't want you to be shot down in some dirty street like Diego was."

Father Rosario was walking behind them.

"She speaks wisely, Marshal," he said. "Violence is not the answer."

"Tell that to Charlotte's father and brother," Shannon said angrily. "What *is* the answer then, Father? What am I supposed to do—turn the other cheek? Rancho Alvarez belongs solely to Charlotte now. If she doesn't sign it over to Kruger, he'll kill her too. I'm not going to let that happen. You can't avoid violence if your enemies insist on thrusting it upon you. I don't know what the next world is like, but in this world you fight or you die. It's as simple as that."

"I'm sorry you feel that way, my son," said the priest.

"So am I, Father," Shannon said. "So am I."

As Shannon and Charlotte approached the house, Pedro Rodriguez joined them.

"What now, *amigo*?" he said. "The *vaqueros* want to ride into Los Santos and wipe out Kruger and his gang once and for all."

"I wish we could do just that," Shannon said, "but it wouldn't be smart to try. We don't have the men for a confrontation like that. If we started a gun battle with Kruger's people on their own ground, we'd be the ones who got wiped out. Besides, we can't leave the hacienda undefended. We'll have to make our fight here."

"Then you think that Kruger will attack the hacienda again?" said Charlotte.

"Yes," Shannon said. "He knows we won't risk bringing you back into town, so he'll have to come after you. He'll attack all right, and soon. Probably tonight."

"Then we must prepare ourselves," said Rodriguez. "What do you suggest?"

As Shannon and Rodriguez were discussing the defense of the hacienda, one of the *vaqueros* came hurrying up to them.

"Your pardon, Señores," he said. "There is a rider approaching the front gate."

"Just one man?" Shannon asked.

"Sí, Señor. One man only."

"Come on, Pete," said Shannon. "Let's see what this is all about."

They stood behind the iron gate, watching the horseman approach.

"It's one of Kruger's people," Shannon said. "Stay alert, everyone."

The man stopped his horse a few yards from the gate, wrapped the reins around the saddle horn, and raised his hands above his head.

"Marshal Shannon!" he called. "It's Red Harper. Can I talk with you for a minute?"

"Open the gate," Shannon said. "I'll see what he wants. Cover me, in case it's some sort of trap."

He went through the gate and walked out to the spot where Harper was waiting. As he drew near, he saw that Harper's face was badly battered. There were cuts and bruises around his eyes and mouth, and there was also a dirty bandage wrapped around his right hand.

"Well?" Shannon said, keeping his hand close to his holster.

"I quit Kruger, Marshal," said Harper. "I'm gettin' out of New Mexico."

"What happened to your face?"

"Kruger's men did it. Snyder and the rest."

"Why?"

"They was mad because I tried to stop 'em from hurtin' that old sheriff," Harper said. "I tried to keep 'em from ambushing you last night outside the church, too, and that made 'em even madder. They knocked me around for a while and then dumped me behind some trash cans in that alley, the same one in which they hid while they were waiting to jump you. I came to and got away before the shooting started."

"That explains the blood spots we found," Shannon said. "But why have you come here today?"

"I know I'm no better than the next man, Marshal," Harper said. "I've earned my living with a gun, sure. But when it comes to beating up old men and killing kids, well, I can't stomach it anymore. I had enough. I'm through with Kruger and all the rest of them."

"You rode a long way just to tell me you quit," said Shannon. "Is that all?"

"No, there's something else," Harper said. "I

wanted to warn you about it, you and the others. Kruger's coming after you. He's planning to hit you tonight with everything he's got. He wants to kill everyone here—men, women, children, everyone. I thought you ought to know."

"I appreciate that, Harper," Shannon said, his voice a little softer now. "You didn't have to do this, and I'm grateful to you."

"That's okay," Harper said. "The Alvarez family, they're decent people. I ain't gonna help Kruger hurt 'em anymore."

"There are a couple of other things I need to know," said Shannon, "if you feel like telling me."

"Okay, Marshal. Whatever you want."

"Did Kruger order the murder of Alejandro Alvarez?"

"Sure," Harper said. "Everybody knows that."

"I had to be certain," Shannon said. "And the ambush last night, when they shot Diego Alvarez?"

"Yeah, that was Kruger's doing. I guess you already knew that anyway. They wanted to get the woman too, but you got them first."

"One more thing," said Shannon. "Who killed the two guards who were on that gate back there the night Kruger's people got into the house?"

"That was Lester, the man you pistol-whipped outside the office the next morning. He got 'em both, and bragged about it afterward, the little weasel. Knifin' a couple of boys in the back ain't nothin' for any man to brag about. Lester's crazy. I expect he'll get what's coming to him one of these days."

Harper took up his reins.

"Anything else, Marshal, before I go on my way?"

"I guess not," Shannon said. "Thanks again, Harper. Good luck to you. Where are you headed?"

"Arizona, maybe. Might try a little prospecting. Anything would be better than workin' for Kruger. Well, so long."

He rode away up the road. Shannon walked back to the gate.

"What did he say?" Rodriguez asked as he closed the gate behind Shannon.

"Kruger's coming after us, all right. Harper says he's sending his men tonight with orders to kill us all."

"Then we must be ready," said Rodriguez. "Let us get on with our preparations."

"There's one other thing, Pete," Shannon said. "Harper confirmed what we already suspected—the man called Lester is the one who killed Carlos and Ernesto."

Rodriguez's face hardened.

"Thank you for telling me," he said. "No matter what else happens, this Lester will pay dearly for what he has done. I swear it on the graves of my poor boys."

Once more, Charlotte sat with Shannon in the garden. The scent of the flowers was as rich as ever, but neither of them noticed it. There were too many unpleasant things to think about.

"Do you think Harper was telling the truth?" Charlotte said.

"Oh, yes," Shannon replied. "Harper's warning just confirms what we already suspected—Kruger's men will attack tonight."

"Can we hold them off?"

"We can try. But if they come in force, and they will, we may not have the firepower to prevent them from taking the house."

"Then I'll die defending it," Charlotte said fiercely. "But I don't want you to die, Clay. I told you last night this was my fight, and it still is. You've done all anyone could ask. Leave Rancho Alvarez now. Take Marshal Rodriguez and go while you still can."

"Not likely," Shannon said. "We'll fight this battle together, Charlotte, win or lose."

"Then let's make certain we win," she said.

They prepared their defenses carefully. Shannon had burlap feed bags filled with sand piled up at intervals around the side and rear walls of the house to form small earthworks. A similar barrier was raised along the verandah at the front of the house. Shannon added some flour barrels for good measure. The shutters of the house were closed and locked. The ranch house had been built in a time when defense against Indians and other marauders was a concern, so the shutters had firing ports through which those inside could shoot. Fortunately, the house sat upon natural springs, the same springs that gave life to the garden, and Charlotte's father years ago had devised a pumping system to provide water to the house and grounds. Hoses were now attached to these pumps in case the attackers attempted to burn down the house or outbuildings.

"We'll try to meet them at the outside walls and gate," Shannon said to the *vaqueros*, "and keep them away from the main house. If we can't, fall back to the earthworks along the sides and rear of the building."

"You will give the signal for that, Señor Shannon?" asked the foreman, Ramón.

"Yes," said Shannon, "if I can. If no signal comes, and you're about to be overrun, move back on your own. You'll have to judge that for yourselves."

"Do we have enough cartridges?" another of the *vaqueros* asked.

"We have a fair amount of ammunition on hand," Shannon told them, "but in a stiff fight it'll go fast. We'll pass out what we have, but the supply isn't unlimited. Make each shot count."

He posted the men as best he could, giving them instructions about what to do to meet the different possible forms of attack.

"We don't know how they'll come at us," he told them. "Be ready for anything. Marshal Rodriguez and I will be at the house. We'll fight from the verandah. That's our last line of defense. If they get by us, Señorita Alvarez will surely die."

An angry murmur arose among the *vaqueros*.

"Many of them will die first," said Ramón, the foreman. "Many. And we will give no quarter, any more than they will give it to us." He pulled out a long knife from his belt. "When the ammunition is gone, there are other methods. I haven't slit a throat in a long time, but I remember how."

The others growled their approval.

When all the preparations had been made, Shannon and Pedro Rodriguez sat down on the verandah to clean their weapons. Shannon decided to attempt the same ploy that Charlotte had tried on him.

"I've been thinking, Pete," Shannon said. "There's no need for you to stay. You've done enough. Go home to Dry Wells. Go home to Maria. I can handle this."

"No you can't," Rodriguez said, checking the cleanliness of his rifle barrel.

"Leave, Pedro. I ask it as a favor to me. Ride out now, before dark."

"Not likely," Pedro Rodriguez said with a little smile. Shannon saw the smile, and remembered that he had used the same words to Charlotte. He wondered if his friend had overheard his conversation with her in the garden. He started to ask, but Rodriguez quickly changed the subject.

"This man Lester," he said, his face darkening. "The one who killed my sons. If he comes tonight, *amigo*, will you leave him to me?"

"He's all yours," Shannon said grimly.

As sundown approached, Shannon and Charlotte Alvarez went through the grounds together, double-checking their precautions.

"When Kruger's men hit us tonight," Shannon said, "it's going to be rough. Odds are some of us aren't going to see the next sunrise. If I'm one of the ones who don't, I want you to know that I have no regrets. I'm glad I came here. I'm glad I met you."

"I'm sorry I've put your life in jeopardy," Charlotte said. "But somehow I can't be sorry you came. We've fought together for what we love and believe in, and

I certainly don't regret that. Whatever happens tonight, I'm content."

"I'm not," Shannon said. "I want to take Kruger down personally and permanently. I just hope I get the chance."

Twilight came and went, but on this evening the lamps were not lit in the Alvarez home. Everyone waited in the darkness, watching, listening, wondering what the next hours would bring.

Shannon could not force himself to sit quietly and wait. He patrolled the grounds restlessly, checking the guards again and again, going over in his mind the hacienda's defenses, trying to think of anything he might have forgotten. There was little else that could be done. On the plus side, they had a few good men, and ample forewarning of an attack. Tactics had been agreed upon, and fighting positions prepared. Another asset was the full moon, for its light would enable them to see the attackers coming—or so Shannon thought. However, at about one o'clock a layer of high clouds moved across the sky, dimming the moonlight and plunging the house and grounds into near-total darkness. Shannon and Rodriguez took their positions on the verandah behind the sandbags and flour barrels they had placed there as cover. They re-checked the readiness of their weapons and waited.

"Any time now," Shannon said.

Minutes later, a distant sound attracted his attention. A wagon was rumbling down the road toward the iron gate. Shannon ran to the gate and looked out. There were no horses pulling the wagon. Someone was pushing it down the slope toward them.

"They're trying to crash the gate," Shannon said. "Get ready, everybody! Ramón, tell your men on the other side of the house to stay put. This may be just a diversion."

He ran back to the verandah.

"It's started," he said to Pedro Rodriguez. "Now we'll see."

The wagon crashed into the gate, breaking it open and lurching through it. Its balance upset by the impact, the vehicle careened to one side and rolled over just inside the grounds. Immediately, shadowy forms came dashing through the opening, firing their weapons. The guards Shannon had posted on either side of the gate returned the fire, and Shannon and Rodriguez began shooting at them as well. More gunfire erupted from the back of the house, and then from the sides.

"Señor Shannon!" Ramón called. "They're climbing over the walls! We can't hold them!"

Shannon raised his rifle and shot a man who had almost reached the verandah steps.

"All right, Ramón," he said. "Bring your men in like we planned."

The Alvarez *vaqueros* retreated back across the grounds, firing at the invaders as they ran. One of them went down as a volley of gun flashes came out of the night. The rest quickly took their places in the positions that had been prepared on each side of the house. Gunfire was everywhere now, and more men were coming over the walls and through the gate.

"How many of these accursed people are there?"

Rodriguez said, knocking one of the intruders off the wall with a well-placed rifle shot.

"Twenty or so, I'd say," said Shannon, downing another man who was approaching the house. "Kruger must have hired some extra guns for this job." He ducked down behind the barrier as several more bullets ploughed into the bags and barrels in front of him. Ramón came running around the side of the house and crouched down beside Shannon.

"We have some of them pinned down in the back," he panted, "but I do not think we will be able to hold them for more than a few minutes. There are too many."

"Keep shooting," Shannon said. "As long as the ammunition lasts, we have a chance." His rifle was now empty, and he slid down behind the barrier to reload it.

"Look, *amigo*," Rodriguez said. "They are sending us another little present."

Shannon saw that a second wagon was coming down the hill. It was filled with bales of hay, and the hay was on fire. The men pushing it leaped aside as the wagon rattled through the ruined gate and rolled onward toward the house. It came past the first wagon, and for a moment it appeared that it would reach the verandah. But Shannon, half-anticipating such an attack, had arranged for large stones to be placed across the front of the verandah, blocking the way. The wheels of the flaming wagon struck the rocks, and it also overturned, spilling its fiery contents around it. The flames leaping up from the burning hay illuminated the facade of the building, and in its fitful light the attackers were clearly visible as they came rushing forward through the grounds.

"A stupid trick," said Rodriguez. "Now we can see them."

"Yes," said Shannon, shooting at the men running at them through the firelight. "Unfortunately, I see a *lot* of them."

An Alvarez *vaquero* came out onto the verandah.

"Ramón!" he cried. "They are at the rear door of the house!"

Ramón cursed colorfully.

"Pull back into the kitchen and fight them from there," he bawled. "You know the plan! Follow it! I'll be right there."

He leaped up and hurried back into the house. Bullets struck the doorframe beside him as he went through and slammed the door.

Three of Kruger's men had reached a large tree that stood only a few yards from the verandah. Using it for cover, they were shooting rapidly at Shannon and Rodriguez. The two lawmen fired back, and one of the attackers fell to the ground. He lay beside the tree, thrashing about and calling loudly for help. Rodriguez silenced him with another well-aimed rifle shot. As Ramón had said, there would be no quarter asked or given on that night.

Someone opened the front door behind them. Charlotte Alvarez was there, holding a double-barreled shotgun.

"Charlotte, get back inside," Shannon said. "You're supposed to stay in the house."

"I'm staying here," Charlotte replied firmly. "Ramón is taking care of things inside."

She knelt beside Shannon and looked out into the firelight, trying to find a suitable target. One of the attackers had left the shelter of the tree and was making a run for the corner of the house. Charlotte fired both barrels of the shotgun, and the man flipped over in mid-stride, his rifle flying into the air as he fell.

"Magnifico!" Rodriguez said approvingly.

Charlotte was busy reloading the shotgun.

"Charlotte," Shannon began, *"please* go. . . ."

"There!" she said as another of Kruger's men tried for the corner of the building. The shotgun bellowed again, bowling the man over as he ran.

Ramón came out of the house, gasping for breath.

"Señorita!" he panted. "They're throwing firebrands at the back wall."

"Have you started the pumps?" Charlotte asked.

"Yes, Señorita," Ramón replied. "But I don't know if. . . ."

A bullet struck him in the neck and he collapsed next to Charlotte. She dropped the shotgun and bent over him, trying to stop the bleeding. Shannon had spotted the muzzle flash. It came from behind the first wrecked wagon, and he fired quickly at it. Someone howled in anguish, and there were no more shots from that direction.

There was now a noticeable slackening of the gunfire in the grounds.

"We're holding them!" Rodriguez said.

"I don't think we've killed that many," Shannon

said, rising to one knee. "Maybe they're running low on cartridges."

"Or maybe they've just had enough of us," Rodriguez said with satisfaction.

One attacker had not given up. He was darting from tree to tree, approaching the verandah. Then he left the trees and charged straight at the spot where Shannon was kneeling.

"I warned you, Shannon," he screeched. "Now I'll gut you like a fish!"

"Pete," Shannon said quietly, "that's Lester, the one who knifed your boys."

"Gracias a Dios!" Rodriguez said. "My prayers have been answered!"

He leaped over the barrier and began to run toward Lester.

"Get back, Pete!" Shannon shouted. But Rodriguez was intent on his longed-for meeting with the murderer of his sons. Lester saw him coming and fired at him. Rodriguez never faltered. Lester fired again, missed again, and then fled into the garden. Rodriguez pursued him through the trees, and they both disappeared from Shannon's view.

Shannon rose to go after them, but Charlotte put her hand on his arm.

"No, Clay," she said. "We need you here. Let Pedro have his vengeance."

Shots echoed from the garden. A shriek could be heard among the bushes, followed by more shots. One last squeal reached Shannon's ears, and then all was silent.

Shannon shook off Charlotte's restraining grasp and

leaped over the barrier. He started toward the garden, but as he did so Pedro Rodriguez came out of the bushes, wiping a knife on his sleeve. His shirt was torn and bloody.

"Lester's?" said Shannon, indicating the knife.

"Yes," said Rodriguez. "He won't be needing it again."

Two more of Kruger's men were fleeing for the gate. Shannon and Rodriguez fired at the same time. One man went down, the other stumbled but then continued forward, dragging one leg behind him. Behind Shannon the shotgun sounded once more, and the second man collapsed in a heap. Charlotte had again hit her mark.

"How's Ramón?" Shannon asked her, watching the trees for further movement.

"The bullet missed the artery," she said. "He'll survive."

"Good," said Shannon. "I hope the same can be said for the rest of us."

For a full minute, Shannon, Rodriguez, and Charlotte Alvarez stood there together, back to back, weapons at the ready, looking around for further opposition. Presently another of the Alvarez men came hurrying out of the house.

"Señorita Alvarez!" he called. "The men who attacked us have run away, but the rear of the house is on fire!"

"In that case," Charlotte said calmly, "don't just stand there, Rafael. Go put it out."

"Yes, Señorita," Rafael said. "We are pumping water on the flames now. But those men are getting away. May we go after them?"

Charlotte looked at Shannon.

"No," Shannon said. "We can't afford to start blundering around in the dark and leaving the house undefended. Just put out the fire, as the Señorita says."

"Very well, Señor," Rafael said. "But next time we will get them all."

He scurried back into the house.

All gunfire had now ceased. Pedro Rodriguez and the Alvarez *vaqueros* began moving through the grounds, checking bodies for signs of life, peering into the bushes to see if any of the attackers were hiding there. One wounded gunman was discovered by Rodriguez himself. It appeared that while fleeing through the darkness, the man had run full-tilt into a tree, knocking himself unconscious. The *vaqueros* reported that no other Kruger men were found alive.

When he was sure it was all over, Shannon took a deep breath and holstered his Colt. Charlotte moved up to stand next to him.

"We did it, Clay," she said. "We won!"

"We're still alive, anyway," Shannon said. "Right now, I'll settle for that."

The fire in the house was extinguished, but not before it had done severe damage to the rear of the building. Two of the Alvarez *vaqueros* had been killed and three were wounded, including the foreman, Ramón. Seven of Kruger's men were found dead on the grounds, another one outside the walls. Shannon noted that some of the deceased attackers had gunshot injuries that might not have proved fatal had it not been for the knife wounds in their bodies. The *vaqueros* had taken their own revenge.

The injured Kruger gunman had recovered consciousness. It was Snyder, the man Shannon had fought with in the livery stable in Los Santos. The *vaqueros* wanted to kill him, but Charlotte ordered them instead to place him in the barn under guard.

"Try to find a particularly dirty stall to put him in," Shannon said as the *vaqueros* led him away. "We want him to feel at home."

There was one other casualty. Charlotte's aunt was found dead in her bed, her maid weeping beside her. Her body showed no sign of a wound.

"It was her heart, I think," the maid sobbed. "It was weak, as you know, Señorita Alvarez. She was very frightened when the shooting began, and it must have been too much for her."

Charlotte sat down by the bed. She lowered her head, and began to cry. Shannon turned away in anguish. All at once he was very, very tired. He left the room and went a few steps down the hallway. There he leaned against the wall and closed his eyes. Exhaustion had drained the anger out of him, but it was immediately replaced by a deep and terrible resolve.

Chapter Thirteen

One by one, the lamps were lit inside the house. By their light, Shannon saw that Pedro Rodriguez had a knife wound in his side. After the bleeding had been stopped, Rodriguez sat stoically as Shannon sewed up the cut with some silk thread from the Alvarez family's sewing cabinet. Then, weakened by the loss of blood, Rodriguez was taken to one of the bedrooms to lie down.

When he was satisfied that his friend was resting comfortably, Shannon went looking for Charlotte. He found her in the sitting room, her head tilted back against the leather padding of her chair. She looked very weary. Shannon sat down next to her.

"Well, Señorita," he said bitterly, "now my failure is complete. You've lost your father, your brother, your aunt, the house, everything."

Charlotte gave him a tired smile.

"Not everything," she said. "Thanks to you, I still have the land and I still have my life. As for the house, it is only damaged, and it will be rebuilt."

"I'm glad," Shannon said. "At least I've denied Kruger something."

"What about Kruger?" said Charlotte. "I didn't see him during the attack. He certainly wasn't among the dead."

"His kind seldom come to the party themselves. They prefer to send others to do the dying for them. Kruger's probably back in Los Santos right now, hiding in a root cellar somewhere. But I'll find him. Wherever he is, I'll find him."

At dawn, Shannon had Snyder, the injured Kruger gunman, brought from the barn. The man stood before them, swaying a little with the after-effects of the concussion. Fear showed on his face.

"What're you gonna do to me, Shannon?" he said. "You ain't gonna shoot me, are you?" His voice was shaking, and so were his hands.

"I'd like to hang you," said Shannon, "but I have another use for you. I'm going to put you on a horse and send you back into town. I want you to deliver a message to Kruger for me."

Snyder looked relieved.

"What . . . what do you want me to say to Kruger?" he said unsteadily.

"Tell him I'm coming into Los Santos tonight. Tell him I'll meet him in the plaza at sundown, just the two of us. And tell him to come armed."

Now that he knew he wasn't going to die, Snyder became bellicose once more.

"Sundown?" he retorted, his lip curling in derision. "Why wait until then? Why not go right now? You scared?"

"I have some friends to bury," Shannon replied evenly, "and I want Kruger to have all day to think about this and squirm. Now get out of my sight before I change my mind and dangle you from the nearest tree."

The man was led out of the room. When he was gone, Charlotte spoke.

"Do you have to do this, Clay?" she asked.

"Yes," Shannon said flatly. "I do. We won the battle last night, but the war is far from over. Kruger still has his ambitions, his hatred, and his hired guns. As long as he's alive, he'll be a threat to you. I can't leave it like that. Besides, I have a rendezvous with our old friend Mr. Kane, and I don't want to disappoint him."

"Kruger won't face you alone, you know. Kane will be there, and whatever's left of Kruger's gang."

"I don't care," Shannon said, "as long as Kruger's there too."

In the light of a glorious sunrise they buried the dead, both friend and enemy. Charlotte's aunt and the Alvarez *vaqueros* were solemnly interred in the Alvarez family cemetery. The corpses of Kruger's men were tossed into a common grave in an arroyo on the far side of a distant hill.

"I'm sorry there was no priest to say the words over your aunt and your men," Shannon said to Charlotte.

"I'll send Father Rosario out when I reach Los Santos this evening."

"Thank you," Charlotte said. "The families of the *vaqueros* will be grateful."

"It won't bring their husbands and fathers back to life, though, will it?" Shannon said, staring at the sun as it rose slowly above the eastern horizon.

That afternoon, Shannon had the buckskin saddled and brought around to the front of the house. He checked the girth as Charlotte watched unhappily from the steps.

"Don't go alone, Clay," she said. "Take Pedro with you, and some of the men."

"No," Shannon said. "Pedro's still asleep, and in any event he shouldn't ride with that knife wound. When he wakes up, don't tell him I've gone. Otherwise he'll try to come after me. As for your people, they're needed here to stand guard."

"I'll go with you, then."

"No you won't," said Shannon, "and this time I mean it. Kruger and Kane are mine. Whatever happens tonight, I'll feel better knowing you're here, out of harm's way."

The buckskin moved nervously, and Shannon stroked its silky neck to reassure it.

"Anyway," he said, "I'd rather nobody else came along. The people who try to help me always get hurt, and I don't want that to happen anymore."

"But you can't do everything by yourself," Charlotte said.

"Oh, yes I can," Shannon said. "Once upon a time,

when I was younger, I always worked alone, and that's how I'm going to work from now on. It's better that way. Then nobody gets hurt—except maybe me."

He mounted the buckskin and smiled down at her.

"Thanks for everything," he said. "Take care of yourself."

"*Vaya con Dios,*" Charlotte whispered. "I'll be praying for you."

"Thanks for that too," Shannon said bleakly. "Goodbye, Señorita Alvarez."

He swung the horse's head around and went out through the shattered gate, riding slowly toward whatever awaited him in Los Santos.

Chapter Fourteen

The sun was nearly touching the western hills as Shannon rode into Los Santos. He knew that someone had been following him for the past several miles, but whoever it was had stayed well back, and Shannon was too intent upon his mission to worry about it. If it was one of Kruger's men, he'd soon know it. If it wasn't, it didn't matter.

As he approached the center of town he heard the sound of voices ahead of him, and saw that firelight was glinting off the buildings that surrounded the plaza. Surely this could not be the dying embers of Kruger's office, for that fire would have burned itself out long ago. Then, as he entered the plaza, Shannon looked around in astonishment. People were lined up all along the sides of the square, two and three deep in places, and many of them were holding burning torches. The flames lit up the entire plaza, casting dancing shadows on the walls of the buildings and bringing out each detail of the plaza in sharp relief. Shannon saw that the crowd was composed of both *Anglos* and *Mexicanos,* standing shoulder to shoulder.

"Come to see blood, I suppose," he said to himself morbidly.

The buzz of voices stopped as the buckskin plodded across the square, and all eyes became fixed upon Shannon. He passed the blackened ruins of the Los Santos Development Company without even a glance and reined up in front of the hotel steps. A young boy was standing by the steps; Shannon dismounted and handed the reins to him.

"Tie him up for me, will you son?" he said, smiling at the boy. "I won't be long."

Another rider was entering the plaza behind him. Shannon was not terribly surprised to see that it was Charlotte Alvarez. She dismounted beside him, meeting his gaze with defiance in her eyes. Clearly she was expecting a rebuke for being there.

Instead, Shannon grinned at her.

"I thought it might be you behind me," he said. "Why is it that every time I ask you to stay out of danger, you follow me into it?"

"I had to come, Clay," she said. "One way or the other, this is the end of it. I want to be here, whatever happens. Surely I'm entitled to that much."

The firelight's reflections danced in her raven hair, and the flickering light and the proud defiance merely made her more beautiful. Shannon realized that he wanted this woman, and realized just as quickly that within the next few minutes a bullet might end his chances of ever having her.

"Believe it or not, Señorita, I'm glad you're here," he said. He gestured at the waiting crowd. "At least I'll have one friend among all these grim faces."

A murmur arose from the throng, and Shannon saw that King Kruger was advancing across the square toward him. He was wearing the same wrinkled white suit, and his features were distorted with anger. Kane followed in his wake, the usual sardonic smile on his lips. Behind them, three of Kruger's hired gunmen trailed along at a disrespectful distance. They did not look as if they were very pleased to be there.

As he neared the spot where Shannon was standing, Kruger glowered around him at the waiting crowd.

"You people!" he shouted. "Go on home! This is none of your business."

No one moved.

"Go home, I said!" Kruger bellowed angrily.

A figure stepped forward out of the crowd. It was Don Ricardo Morales.

"No, Señor Kruger," Don Ricardo said in a firm voice. "We will not go home. We do not take orders from you anymore."

"Oh yeah?" Kruger said. "You and your pals seem to have forgotten that what I say around here goes. You better remember that if you want that young granddaughter of yours to stay alive."

"My granddaughter is no longer in Los Santos, Señor Kruger," said Morales quietly. "She and my wife are now in a place of safety below the border, far beyond your reach. Your threats mean nothing to me now."

Morales nodded to Shannon.

"Forgive me for not joining you sooner, Señor Shannon," he said. "I had to wait until I was sure that my grandchild was safe before I came forward. Now I am free to act, and, as you see, I have brought some of my fellow citizens with me."

"They're most welcome, Don Ricardo," Shannon said. "So are you."

"I'll take care of you later, Morales," Kruger snarled. "You can bet on it. Right now I got business with Shannon—business he won't like."

"I'm surprised to see you here, Kruger," Shannon said. "I thought your specialty was hiding under a rock somewhere while other people did your dirty work. You must be pretty confident to stick your nose out into the open air like this. I wonder why."

Before Kruger could respond to this, Sheriff Wagner came into the plaza, accompanied by several men whom Shannon recognized from the meeting at the church. All of them were carrying rifles, revolvers, or machetes. They were herding four of Kruger's hired guns ahead of them. Snyder was one of the four. The Kruger men looked crestfallen, and their holsters were empty.

"He was confident, all right," Wagner said, waving his six-gun at the four disarmed gunmen. "A few of us did some advance scouting, and we found these skunks hiding on the rooftops with rifles, waiting to drygulch you right here in the plaza. Guess we spoiled your surprise, didn't we Kruger?"

Shannon regarded Kruger with contempt.

"Well, Kruger," he said, "I'm glad to see that you're acting true to form, right to the very end."

He turned and smiled approvingly at Wagner.

"Thanks, Ed," he said. "Now you're a real lawman at last."

Wagner grinned broadly.

"Keep 'em covered, boys," he said to the men behind him. "If they move, plug 'em. I'll list 'em as 'shot while trying to escape.' "

Kruger was nearly dancing with rage.

"You'll be sorry for this, Wagner," he fumed. "You've crossed me for the last time. I'll have my boys rip your stupid head off."

"Shut up, Kruger," Shannon said. "Your killing days are over. You're finished."

"Yeah?" Kruger sneered. "What makes you think so?"

"I'm calling you out," Shannon said. "Right here, right now. Just the two of us, face to face, man to man—if you are a man, which I doubt. I'd like to kill you where you stand, but because I represent the law I'll give you a choice. You can surrender to me and toss that pistol you're wearing into the dirt, or you can draw it and die, right in front of all these people you've abused for so long. Well, which will it be?"

Kruger's face paled.

"Kane," he said, "do something!"

Kane stepped up beside Kruger, sweeping his coat back to reveal his holstered six-gun.

"First you and I have something to settle between us, Shannon," he said, his yellow eyes glittering in the firelight. "We always knew it would come to this. Next to myself, you're the fastest man with a gun I've ever met. Now we're going to find out which one of us is the fastest."

"This isn't necessary, Kane," Shannon said.

"Yes it is," Kane replied. "And don't try to avoid it by refusing to draw on me. I'm going to count to three. If you haven't pulled that Colt by the time I say 'three,' I'll kill you anyway."

Shannon sighed.

"All right," he said. "Let's get it over with. Any time you're ready," Kane started counting.

"One," he said. "Two. Thr. . . ."

A gunshot echoed in the plaza. Kane staggered back, staring in astonishment at the spreading stain in the center of his shirt. Then he fell over on his face in the dust of the street.

Shannon had never touched his gun. Startled by the shot, he whirled around to see who had fired. Charlotte Alvarez was standing on the boardwalk a few feet away from him, her arm held straight out before her and the little silver .32 revolver in her hand. A wisp of smoke was still curling from the muzzle.

"Why, Charlotte?" Shannon said. "I could have outdrawn him."

"Possibly," Charlotte said, slipping the .32 back into her jacket. "But I couldn't take the chance."

Dismayed, Shannon knelt beside Kane and rolled him over. Kane was still conscious, but his life was ebbing quickly from the wound in his chest.

"I'm sorry, Kane," Shannon said. "I didn't know she was going to do that."

Kane gave Shannon one of his mysterious smiles.

"It's all right, Shannon," he said, coughing. "You might have beaten me anyway."

"I doubt it," Shannon said. "You're the best I've ever seen. I think you would have taken me."

Kane coughed again. A trickle of blood ran down from the corner of his mouth.

"Thanks for saying that," he whispered, "even if you don't believe it. I guess we'll never know now, will we? Take good care of that woman, Shannon. She's something really special. I only wish . . ."

His voice trailed away. He took one last ragged breath and died.

King Kruger had been standing nearby, watching in disbelief. His face was now chalk white.

"Shoot that woman!" he screamed to the hired gun-hands waiting behind him. "Shannon too!"

The three gunmen hesitated. Don Ricardo Morales stepped off the boardwalk and stood beside Shannon in the street.

"No, Señores," he said loudly. "You will not harm Señor Shannon or Señorita Alvarez. The first one of you who draws a gun will die at our hands. As you see, we are well armed, and we will shoot if necessary."

Shannon saw that it was true. More than a dozen of the citizens of Los Santos had moved out of the crowd; they all had firearms and were pointing their weapons at Kruger's men, ready to cut them down.

The gunmen moved their hands carefully away from their holsters.

"Take it easy," one of them said. "We don't want no trouble. We're as sick of Kruger as you are."

"Very well," said Morales. "*Compadres,* take their weapons."

Men came forward and removed the Kruger men's revolvers from their holsters.

"Bring up their horses," Morales called.

Three more townsmen came out of a side street, each leading several horses.

"As you see, gentlemen" Morales said, "We have prepared ourselves for this moment. We have brought all of your mounts from Kruger's livery stable, and we have placed your saddles on them. Get on the horses and ride out of Los Santos immediately." He motioned to the men that Wagner had rounded up and disarmed earlier. "That applies to the four of you also," he said. "Go now, and consider yourselves fortunate. I suggest that all of you keep riding at least until you reach the New Mexico border."

"Yeah, we'll go," said one of the Kruger men. "We're fed up with this town anyway. What about our guns?"

"The guns stay here," Morales said. "If you return, we will kill you with them."

Uttering muffled curses, the gunmen sorted out their horses, mounted up, and galloped full-tilt out of the plaza. Their hoofbeats faded away into the night.

Kruger started to move toward one of the remaining horses.

Shannon, who had been a fascinated spectator to all of this, quickly barred his way.

"Not you," Shannon said. "You stay here. You're

all alone now, Kruger, with nobody to do your killing for you. I'm placing you under arrest for murder."

Kruger backed away, his eyes bulging in fright.

"Let me go, Shannon," he pleaded. "I'll get out of town and you'll never see me again."

"Not a chance," Shannon said. "You're going to stand trial for the crimes you've committed. You're going to hang, Kruger, and I plan to slip the noose over your head myself."

Kruger let out a wail of pure terror and went for his holster. Shannon drew the Colt and fired in one smooth motion. Kruger squawked like a frightened chicken and dropped his six-gun, clawing at his right arm. There was blood on the white sleeve where Shannon's bullet had torn through the flesh.

"I could have killed you, Kruger," Shannon said, "but I'm saving you for the gallows. Now let's go. Your jail cell is waiting."

"No!" Kruger whimpered, looking around wildly at the crowd. "These people hate me. They'll kill me if you put me in the jail."

Shannon realized that for once Kruger was telling the truth. The people of Los Santos were edging forward toward Kruger with murder in their eyes.

"Stop!" Shannon said, stepping between the crowd and Kruger. "Don't do it! You're good and decent people, but if you kill this man now, like this, you'll be no better than he is. Let the law take care of Kruger."

"Listen to the Marshal!" Morales said.

"Kruger has beaten and robbed us and killed our friends," someone shouted. "He deserves to die."

"He'll die all right," Shannon said, "but only after a proper trial."

"Look, Señor Shannon!" Don Ricardo exclaimed. "He's getting away!"

Shannon turned and saw that Kruger, taking advantage of Shannon's momentary distraction with the crowd, had bolted through the circle of onlookers and was running out of the plaza.

Somewhat exasperated with himself for allowing his man to flee, Shannon holstered his six-gun and started striding purposefully after Kruger. Morales came with him. The crowd followed, shouting and waving their torches.

"Alas, Señor Shannon," Morales said. "He's escaped."

"No he hasn't," Shannon said. "I saw where he went. He ran into the church. You keep all these people back out of the way. I'll get him."

Shannon climbed the steps of the church and pushed open the heavy door. Once inside, he halted abruptly. Kruger was cowering in front of the altar, his features contorted with fear and malice. He was holding Father Rosario in front of him, and he had a small four-barreled pistol pressed hard against the priest's temple.

"Don't try anything, Shannon," he said. "If you do, I'll kill your saintly friend here."

"I might have known you'd have a hideout gun," Shannon said. "It's just your style."

He drew the Colt and started forward.

"Give it up, Kruger," he said harshly. "Drop the pistol or I'll drop you."

"Stop it, both of you," said Father Rosario. "There

must be no killing here. Not in the church, before the altar of God. That would be an unforgivable sin. Leave, Señor Shannon, I beg of you. Go, before something terrible happens."

"Do what he says, Shannon," Kruger said, crouching down behind Father Rosario and digging the muzzle of the pistol harder into the side of the priest's head. "If you don't, I'll blow his brains out."

Shannon weighed the odds and decided that he would have to comply. Kruger was almost entirely hidden behind Father Rosario, and the hammer of his little pistol was cocked. The short-barreled pistol was an inaccurate weapon, but with its muzzle already against the priest's head, Kruger couldn't fail to inflict a mortal wound. Shannon knew that he might be able to get a bullet into the part of Kruger's body that was visible, but in the dim light, with such a small target, he could well miss. And even if he didn't miss, Kruger might still pull the trigger of the pistol before he went down, killing Father Rosario. As much as he wanted to finish Kruger, Shannon realized that he couldn't take that chance with Father Rosario's life.

"All right, Kruger," he said in a tired voice. "You win—for now. But sooner or later you'll have to release the priest and leave the mission, and when you do, I'll be waiting. There's no place you can run to, no place you can hide, that I won't find you. You'll be looking over your shoulder the rest of your life, and one day I'll be there."

He spun on his heel and strode back down the aisle to the entrance of the church. He opened the door, then paused and looked back.

"You're slime, Kruger," he said. "I've been a lawman for twenty years, and I've never come across a fouler, more disgusting piece of filth than you. You make me want to vomit. The next time I see you, I'll gun you down without a moment's hesitation."

He walked out of the church and slammed the door.

The crowd had gathered in front of the church, waiting expectantly. Charlotte was among them. As Shannon came out, she ran up to him.

"What happened, Clay?" she said. "Did Kruger get away?"

"No," Shannon said, "but he's holding Father Rosario hostage, and I had to back off to save the Father's life. Don't worry, I'll get Kruger later."

Behind him the front door of the church flew open and Kruger came stumbling out, still holding the priest in front of him. There was madness in his face.

"Nobody talks to me like that, Shannon!" he screamed. "I'm gonna kill you right now! You and that Alvarez witch!" His eyes were wild, and spittle flew from his open mouth.

"No, Señor Kruger!" exclaimed Father Rosario, "You mustn't harm them! You mustn't!"

He twisted his body around, trying to grapple with Kruger. Kruger cursed and pulled the trigger of the little pistol. The muzzle flash momentarily lit up the front of the church, and Father Rosario crumpled onto the steps. Charlotte Alvarez cried out and started toward the fallen priest.

Kruger raised the pistol and aimed it at her.

"I've got you now," he shrieked. "I've got you now, you. . . ."

With his left hand, Shannon reached out and pushed Charlotte to the ground. With his right hand he drew his six-gun. The flickering torchlight gleamed on the barrel.

Kruger fired just as Shannon moved. The bullet passed between Charlotte and Shannon, missing Charlotte by a fraction of an inch. Kruger was struggling clumsily with the hammer of the pistol, trying to cock it for another shot. Shannon raised the Colt and fired. The heavy .45 slug sent Kruger flying backwards, his arms outflung. His body landed heavily, spreadeagled on the stone steps.

Shannon bent over Charlotte Alvarez.

"Are you hurt?" he asked, his fear for her apparent in his voice.

Charlotte got to her feet, clinging to Shannon's arm.

"I'm all right, Clay," she said. "He missed me. But Father Rosario—is he dead?"

Shannon hurried up the steps to the place where Father Rosario was lying. As he approached, the priest sat up, holding one hand to the side of his head. His face was scorched from the muzzle blast of Kruger's pistol, and his cheek was covered with blood.

"Don't worry about me, Marshal," Father Rosario said in an unsteady voice. "I dodged away just in time. What about Kruger?"

Shannon went over to the fallen man. Kruger was clutching at his abdomen where Shannon's bullet had struck him. It was obvious that the wound was mortal.

"You've ruined everything, Shannon," Kruger wheezed. "I could have ruled the world if you hadn't come along. I could have been an emperor, like Bonaparte and Caesar. That was my dream, and you've spoiled it."

"There's something you should know," Shannon said. "I've been meaning to mention it to you. Napoleon Bonaparte died a prisoner on a tiny island in the South Atlantic. His jailers poisoned him. As for Julius Caesar, he was stabbed to death by his own friends one day as he entered the Roman senate. Your mad ambitions have brought you only death, Kruger, just as their ambitions brought death to Bonaparte and Caesar. You've got that much in common with them, at least."

Kruger glared up at him.

"I'll kill you, Shannon," he croaked. "I'll . . . kill . . . you!"

He fumbled for the four-barreled pistol which was lying beside him on the steps. Shannon picked up the weapon and tossed it aside.

"I'm sick of your threats, Kruger," Shannon said. "I told you before—your killing days are over."

Kruger uttered one last gurgle of hate, then fell back dead.

Shannon turned and went back down the steps. Father Rosario knelt beside Kruger's body and began to administer the last rites.

Chapter Fifteen

As the dawn broke over Rancho Alvarez, Pedro Rodriguez took the reins and mounted his horse. Shannon, who was standing beside him, saw that Rodriguez grimaced in pain as he climbed into the saddle.

"I wish you'd stick around for a few more days, Pete," Shannon said. "That cut could use a little more time to heal."

"No, my friend," said Rodriguez. "Maria needs me. I must tell her about our sons. All that she's had is a telegram, and she deserves better. I must go."

"I understand," Shannon said. "When you get home, don't forget to have Maria take those stitches out."

Rodriguez chuckled.

"I may keep them as a souvenir of our little adventure in New Mexico," he said. "But what about you, *amigo*? I trust you will remain here?"

Shannon shook his head.

182

"No," he said, "I'm leaving."

"Leaving Los Santos? What about Señorita Alvarez?"

"She doesn't need me anymore," Shannon said in a hollow voice.

Pedro Rodriguez raised one eyebrow.

"Are you sure about that?" he said.

"Yes," Shannon replied. "My work here is finished."

"But what will you do? Where will you go?"

"Perhaps to California. It's growing rapidly, and lawmen will be needed there."

"Lawmen are needed everywhere," Rodriguez said, "including New Mexico. Men like us never lack for work, no matter where we are."

"That's true," said Shannon. "Unfortunately."

He stepped back away from the horse.

"So long, Pete," he said. "Will you give my regards to Maria?"

"Certainly," Rodriguez said. "And she will send hers to you. Will you come to visit us in Dry Wells?"

"Perhaps someday," Shannon said. "If I can."

"You will always be welcome," said Rodriguez, reaching down to shake Shannon's hand. "But I must go now, for I have a long journey ahead of me. *Adios,* my friend."

He rode away through the broken gate and up the dusty road. At the top of the hill he stopped and raised his arm in one last salute. Then he turned his horse and slowly disappeared from view.

* * *

Once again Shannon and Charlotte Alvarez walked together in the garden.

"It's over, Charlotte," Shannon said. "You're safe. Your father and brother are avenged, and you can get on with your life."

"You made it possible, Clay," she said. "I'm very grateful."

"I just wish I could have done more," said Shannon.

"You've done a great deal," Charlotte said. "For one thing, you saved Los Santos. Its people are free now, and they will never again allow someone like Kruger to exploit or abuse them."

"I may have saved Los Santos," Shannon said glumly, "But I'm afraid I didn't save much else." He glanced over his shoulder at the blackened timbers at the rear of the house.

"Yes, you did, Clay," said Charlotte. "You saved Rancho Alvarez, and you saved me. I've been able to hire many more people now, and tomorrow we begin rebuilding the house. In two or three months, it will be restored to its former beauty."

"That's good news," Shannon said. "Perhaps I'll return one day to see it, if you'll allow me."

Charlotte took his arm, holding it tightly against her. When she spoke, her voice almost broke with emotion.

"Don't return, Clay," she said. "Stay instead."

"Stay?" said Shannon.

"Yes," Charlotte said. "Stay here with me. I'm alone now. I need someone to share my land and my life with me. Stay and help me rebuild. You spoke once of changes coming, of prosperity and statehood. Stay and share them with me. Share Rancho Alvarez with me. It needs you as much as I do."

Shannon did not speak for several moments, as he weighed what Charlotte had just said. There was nothing for him anywhere else. His wife and son were gone, and the town of Whiskey Creek was silent and empty by now. He had no ties anywhere—except here, to this land and to this woman.

Someone came into the garden behind them. It was Ramón, the Alvarez foreman. His throat was bandaged but otherwise he seemed to have suffered no ill effects from his wound.

"Your pardon, Señor Shannon," he said deferentially, "but your horse is at the front door of the house, saddled as you asked, with your saddlebags upon his back."

"Thanks, Ramón," Shannon said absently. "Wait just a moment, will you?"

He looked down at Charlotte's upturned face.

"It will be quite a challenge, won't it?" he said. "Rebuilding the place, meeting the future here?"

"A great challenge," she said. "And I can't face it all by myself."

"Yes, you can," said Shannon with a sorrowful little smile.

"Well, I don't *want* to face it by myself," Charlotte said. "I want us to face it *together*."

She reached up to him, wrapping her arms around his neck. Her body was soft against his, and her kiss was long and inviting.

After several moments Shannon became aware that someone was watching them. He looked up and saw that Ramón was still there, waiting, a broad grin on his face.

"You can put the buckskin away, Ramón," Shannon said. "I won't be needing him for quite awhile."

Clay Shannon was no longer alone.